the queen of ebenezer

by k. b. hoyle

OWL'S NEST PUBLISHERS

OWL'S NEST
PUBLISHERS

Est. 2021
Owl's Nest Publishers
P. O. Box 63
Cross Plains, WI 53528
owlsnestpublishers.com

Cover Images: Michelle Moran Copyright © 2023, @DAPA
Images via Canva
Cover Design: Ash Schlax, K. B. Hoyle
Title Font: by Ash Schlax
Text Font: Rumba, Didot

ISBN: 978-1-957362-24-3 (hardcover)

The Queen of Ebenezer / by K. B. Hoyle
When Beatrice wakes in a magical swamp called Ebenezer, she's
met with the baffling wit and curious whims of the swamp's
single other human inhabitant, the boy "king," Tom.

Printed in the United States of America

the queen of ebenezer

by K. B. Hoyle

also by K. B. Hoyle

for the dreamers

"Here I raise my Ebenezer;
hither by thy help I've come;
and I hope, by thy good pleasure,
safely to arrive at home."

Robert Robinson

owls and night journeys

I followed the owl. That's when all my curiosities began.

I would not ordinarily have followed an owl at night into a dark forest—I have far too much sense for that—but this was no ordinary owl, and it was no ordinary night.

It was a night filled with darkness.

Aren't nights always filled with darkness, you ask?

Yes, but not *this* sort of darkness. This was a darkness I've never felt before. A screaming darkness. A darkness to swallow the world.

This was the night I followed the owl.

Neither was the forest ordinary, but at that time I didn't know.

The forest was on the edge of a swamp.

And the swamp was—

I would not remember the owl until later.

But, as I put one foot in front of the other and walked into the swaying pines and grey elms that swallowed me up, I had only one clear thought in my somnolent mind:

Follow the owl.

my island

I cross a winding creek, I think. Seven white stones.

My feet touch each one for a fleeting moment, but my eyes stay riveted on tawny feathers and a wingspan that is little more than a shadow against an inky sky. My skirt whispers through grass as tall as my knees, my chest (I raise my arms), my knees again. Then I reach a stretch of water as flat, pale, and smooth as a looking glass. In its center is a small mound of perfect green. An island.

My island.

I have arrived.

Gathering my skirt, I wade into the water, disturbing it into silver ripples. When I get to the swell of land, the warm water rolls off my calves and down my ankles and bare feet to meet blades damp with dew. White lilies rise up in a fairy ring, growing and unfurling from the earth, waking and stretching to greet the moon. *Or me.* I trail my fingers along the flowers and smile.

"Well, I've come," I say, not knowing to whom I speak. Now that I've arrived, the owl is nowhere in sight.

The moon shines bright on my patch of earth—for I do feel that it is *my* place—and the softness of night weighs down on my shoulders.

I'm alone.

Hunched over my knees, expecting to feel...

Afraid?

But fear doesn't come. The night presses me down, so I curl onto my side in the warm dewy grass and blink.

This place is heavy with slumber. "I'll just close my eyes for a moment," I say, speaking again to the water, the flowers, the moon, I guess. Away in the trees, in the depths of the far reaches of the swamp, a faint knocking.

Knock,
knock,
knock.

My muscles relax into the earth.

here

I wake slowly.

My face, pressed to the damp grass. My white gown, sticky with sweat to my long legs—legs that brought me here...when? I can't remember.

Maybe I've always been here.

But I can't say I've ever woken up in a swamp before, and that seems like a contradiction, somehow. Or maybe it's a memory.

I sit up all at once, suddenly wide-awake. The air is hot and sort-of heavy, but not a hard-to-breathe heavy. The ground beneath my legs and pressing hands is warm. Birds I can't see call back and forth, back and forth above my head.

A conversation.

I unstick my frilly white cotton gown from my legs. Why I am in a gown in a swamp I cannot say. Yet here I am, and here it is, and it's not even dirty, despite my night on the ground.

With an unsteady lurch, I stand and wriggle my toes. "Bare feet," I say to the bare earth. I peer at them, barely balancing first on one foot and then on the next, expecting to find some scratch or injury or blemish. But I find no hurt, and no clue or hint of what is happening.

Have I always been here, or did I just arrive? I shake my head. The birds have fallen silent, as if the whole swamp is holding its breath with me.

I huff and flip my hair out of my face. Hair that has scrunched into tight honeyed curls that crowd my cheeks and crown my head and flop over into my eyes, making me certain I am not in a dream. If I were dreaming, surely my subconscious wouldn't have produced such humidity.

So, if this is not a dream, then what am I to do?

My stomach gives a mighty growl.

Or eat, for that matter. What does one eat for breakfast in a swamp, anyway? *Have I done this before?*

There is nothing to eat here, unless I conjure it out of thin air. *Will I die in this swamp? Am I dead already?* I laugh that away. "The dead aren't hungry," I say to the breeze.

A tingle—a shiver—runs down my spine, a sensation of people watching me. Whispers from an audience I cannot see.

I turn

and turn

and turn again—but the only voice is my own.

Leaving my island with its ring of white flowers, I gather the hem of my skirt in my long, strong fingers and step lightly into the shallow, still water.

There might be anything there, here, beneath my feet. But still, I step. I feel the bottom of this swampy mire where anything might pinch my toes or bite my heel—but everywhere, the ground is soft, giving way beneath my feet like pillows. After a few cautious steps, I walk easier and cast my eyes upward.

The light is not blue or white, as I expect, but pale green. The trees lumber over me like tall, spindly, leafy people. Trunks twist and grope for the sky, and their leaves filter all the light into a soft, green glow. Cottony puffballs meander past, sparkling like tiny dancers

6

between the quilt-work of the canopy. Beyond, there is blue sky and distant white clouds.

"Oh," I breathe. The loveliness makes me at home; the hominess puts me at peace. This is a place I love.

But…how?

I brush against a hanging vine, and pale yellowish-white flowers unfurl like curling ribbons. A cloying scent fills the air.

Sustenance.

"Honeysuckle!" I laugh and pluck a single bloom— not enough to fill me, but perhaps something to satiate me until I find something real to eat.

Something real. What is real if not this? Putting the flower between my lips, I suck the nectar and carry on.

The light shifts as I walk, sharpening as the honeyed nectar flows into me, widening my eyes, focusing my gaze. Electric blue dragonflies dart back and forth like lightning in the air, frogs and toads hop close to stare, whispers follow me from the trees above, and away in the leaves a lumbering shadow moves—a shadow like a crane, but far too large. I gulp, enamored and somehow not afraid. I drop my skirt to trail in the water.

The nectar is a warm elixir in my veins, propelling me forward, and I grasp the trees to steady myself, every tree I touch buzzing to life under my fingers.

I'm no longer hungry.

Ahead, a path above the water emerges—a path of wood bark and dirt lined with tufts of the greenest grass I've ever seen.

Above, an owl with many eyes swoops low over me. *An owl I've seen before?* I can't remember.

I reel and climb onto the path, pulling myself up like

7

a child onto a tall counter. And there I sit with my head in my hands, waiting for the swamp to stop spinning.

After no time or all the time left in the day, I uncover my face and blink at the world.

The path stretches on in either direction until it disappears into twists and bends in the trees, through the reaching plants that grow from the water all around. Sitting at one end, as still as stones, are a mouse and a squirrel who look very much like they want to say hello.

I laugh, once, a loud guffaw. The mouse and the squirrel jump and scamper off into the trees together. And then I feel sorry, for I would have liked someone to talk to, and I don't know why it shouldn't have been a mouse and a squirrel.

With a wobble, I get to my feet and plant my hands on my hips. I might as well follow this path, wherever it leads. What are paths for, if not for following? I'm confused, but not as confused as I think I should be. And I think I should be afraid, but I can't yet put my finger on what it is, exactly, I should be afraid of.

So instead, I start to walk.

After just a few steps, however, I freeze. Gliding toward me across the water, its body forming a glistening, undulating S, is a snake the color of mud. I catch my breath and stare, gripping my skirt in hands suddenly clammy. *A snake*, and a venomous one at that, with eyes intent on me. And there's nothing between us but the rise of the edge of the path—no barrier to protect me from harm.

I take a shaky step backward, into the far green grass, but still the snake advances. It slides in a rapid curve around a lily pad, raises its head to taste the air—

8

A wooden staff swings down and *whack*, the snake takes a blow and water sprays up around it. I stumble and fall.

A boy. A boy about my age stands there, holding the staff and wrestling with the snake.

"You'll *not*, Ichabod," he says. "No, you'll not!" With a quick motion, he pulls the snake up by its tail and brandishes it, a wide smile on his face. "You don't need to be afraid of old Ichabod—he has to obey me."

the king

The boy gives the snake whose name is Ichabod a gentle shake and then tosses him ten feet away into the water. Ichabod curls into an indignant pile of hissing loops against the bole of a half-submerged tree and stares at us with baleful eyes.

"He *what*?" I say, gathering my feet under me. The boy makes no move to help me stand. "But he's a snake. Why should he obey anyone, let alone you?"

"Because I'm the king of Ebenezer, and I say he does."

This does not clarify a thing. "You're the king of where? *Who* are you?"

The boy clasps his hands behind his back and comes very close to me, leaning down until we are nose-to-nose. His skin is golden brown and he has dark freckles strewn across his nose and upper cheeks. His eyes are a striking greenish amber that somehow match the swampy water, set wide beneath a mop of tightly curled, deep brown hair. His lips are elfin, as if they could not be bothered to stay in a straight line. But beneath his natural smile lurks something...*else*. Something sad, I think. His face seems like this place—wild, whimsical, fantastical—and at once brand new and as familiar to me as my very self.

"Ebenezer," he says, breaking eye contact and moving away. He swings his arms wide. "Ebenezer is here. It's my place. Everything here does what I tell it to."

"*I* don't."

He spins back around, a twinkle in his curious eyes. "No, I suppose you don't, and I don't suppose you will. But you are new to the hereness of it."

A laugh bubbles up and out. "What?"

"Ebenezer. You're new to Ebenezer."

"Then why don't you just say it like that?"

"I just did."

I cross my arms and cant my head. What a peculiar boy.

He mimics my stance. "What if I made you the queen?"

"What do you mean?"

"The queen of here. Would you like to be the queen of Ebenezer?"

"I'm not a queen—I'm just a girl! And I don't think you're a king, either."

"Says who?"

"Says…the rules of…the world!"

"What world? This is the world and I make the rules."

"I…well…" I dart a glance at Ichabod the snake, but he hasn't moved from his coiled position at the base of the swamped tree. He narrows his snakey eyes, and I narrow my eyes in return. I huff and sigh.

"Just say yes, and it will be so," the boy says.

"Okay…" I drag my gaze back to him. "Yes, then. I guess. Why not?"

The boy's face splits wide into a grin, the sort that shows all his teeth right back to the molars. The sort that is infectious. I can't help but return it.

But the snake by the tree hisses in an exasperated

sort of way and uncoils to slide away.

"Hoy, Ichabod!" says the boy, pointing. "Take note of my new queen! Tell the others."

"What are you *doing*?" I laugh on my outburst of words. "He's just a snake. He can't understand you."

The boy turns innocent, serious eyes on me. "All living things understand, down to the roots of the trees where even the water struggles to reach. He must be told," he says. "And now that you're Queen, you will understand, too."

"If you say so, *Your Majesty*."

My joking deference seems to please the boy, who gives me a deep bow and a keen half-smile as the snake disappears into the swamp grass.

"But what is your name?" I say. "You do have a name, don't you? You don't go around asking people to call you King Ebenezer?"

"What people?"

"You know...everyone else." But I'm suddenly struck with the knowledge that there are no other people here. It's just me and him and the other *living things*, whatever they may be, other than the animals and plants. A tinge of fear not unlike the fear of Ichabod claws at my chest, but I swallow it down and square up to the boy. I'm not afraid of this place or this boy or this warm path in the honey-gold light, but the unknown lurking things...they might terrify me yet.

"My name?" The boy furrows his brow and retreats into a spot of shadow on the path. For a moment, the swamp descends into darkness as clouds scuttle across the sky on a quick breeze, and I tip my chin up to study the canopy far above.

Then the boy steps to my side and looks me up and down, from forehead to toes. "Why are you in a dress?" he asks.

I cross my arms against his scrutiny. "It's not a dress—it's a nightgown. And I don't know why. It's just what I woke up in this morning when I was *here*, in"—I try the word on, testing how it rolls off my tongue—"in Ebenezer."

"You can wear anything you'd like here," he says. "Anything at all. Just wish it so and it will be."

"Then why do you dress like that?" I say and eye his ragged jeans, cuffed high on his ankles, his bare feet, and his plain white t-shirt with a single pocket.

He covers the t-shirt pocket with a hand over his heart like I have wounded him. "These are *my* clothes," he says. His eyes slide out of focus just a little. "Clothes for summer hot—for resting in my favorite spot."

I wrinkle my nose.

The light returns to his expression like he's waking up.

"We really should introduce ourselves," I say, hoping again to learn his name. "My name is Beatrice. What's yours?"

To my relief, he looks quickly around and then says, "Tom."

"Nice to meet you, Tom." I stick out my hand.

The boy looks deep into my eyes for a long moment and then slaps his hand into mine. With a vigorous pump, Tom says, "Come on! If you're to be the queen of Ebenezer, you ought to know your way around."

ebenezer

"How did you know—" I say, and then stop. Tom has my hand in his and it's somehow not uncomfortable at all. We fit together like old friends, our fingers finding the comfortable grooves and pressure of a clasp accustomed to use.

"How did I know what?" He glances at me, a glint of sunlight through shallow water.

"Um, how did you know I've never been here before?" I ask, then I blush, because that's really a strange question. "What I mean is—*I* didn't know I've never been here before, when I woke up this morning."

Tom tugs us through a press of green leaves overhanging the path and says, "Easy. I know everything that goes on in Ebenezer."

"*Everything?*"

He freezes like a rabbit hiding from a fox and I collide with him. With chin tilted up and eyes closed, he looks like he's smelling the air, but beneath his lids his eyes roam back and forth. "Listen," he says. "Can you hear them?"

"What?" My whisper falls like dew on the path between us.

"The sweet gum is upset that the woodpecker has made a new nest in her trunk. She wants me to do something about it."

"She...wants you—"

"And away to the west, Eli has fallen asleep after a lunch of minnows from the deepest part of the pool." A

14

smile tilts his lips. "He's snoring."

"Who's Eli?"

"And Dinah cools her wings in the shadow of the sycamore. Minerva watches…"

"Yes?"

He opens his eyes. "You. Minerva watches you. *Just* you. That's odd."

"Is it?" I glance at the green-jeweled canopy far above, but I see no sign of anyone watching me.

Tom drops my hand with a quick laugh and ducks off the path, disappearing deftly into the underbrush.

"*Hey*," I say, and then I shiver. With a look over my shoulder, I find the snake, Ichabod, curled and hanging from a nearby tree.

Ichabod's tongue flickers out, tasting the air. He stares at me, and I stare back until I say, "Didn't Tom give you a job to do?" Then my cheeks flush with the silliness of it—*talking to a snake.* "Go on, now," I say, a little louder. "You can't hurt me."

With effort, I turn my back on Ichabod, just in time for Tom to reappear—like a thought—back on the path.

"Here are two friends," he says, and he places a mouse on my shoulder and a squirrel on my head.

"Oh—*oh!*" I gasp and laugh as the squirrel roots in my mess of curls and the mouse puts its paws on my cheeks, sniffing my skin with its velveteen nose. "You can't just put animals on people without warning!"

"Why not?" Tom tucks his hands into his armpits and rocks onto his heels. "I heard them on the lily pad by the bubbling spring, talking about you. They wanted to meet you earlier but were too shy."

"So that's why you just…ran off. You ran off to get a

mouse and a squirrel. To meet me."

Tom bounds forward and grabs my hands to extend them flat, before me. "Not just any mouse and squirrel. This is Shiloh"—the squirrel scampers off my head and into one of my outstretched hands—"and Archibald." The mouse takes up a perch in the other hand. "They are our special friends."

"Can they"—I glance from the curious creatures to Tom—"talk?"

"If you know how to listen."

"Oh, well. Hi, then."

Shiloh and Archibald tip their heads like twin dolls on a string, and then look at each other and hop in tandem to the ground.

"I didn't hear them say anything. Was I supposed to hear something?"

"They said you're peculiar."

"*Oh*. Well, then—"

"But they think you have a friendly smell."

I want to be offended, but all I can do is giggle. "What does a friendly smell *smell* like?" I ask, hurrying after Tom, who has continued down the path, hands in his pockets.

"Like lavender and fresh cotton that's been dried in the sun over new-cut grass," he says. "And danger and excitement and fire and, and, and—"

"Yes?"

Tom has stopped, head tilted to the side, eyes unfocused at the sky. A distant hollow

beep,
beep,
beep,

16

chases his words but then he says, "That's what you smell like. Come on."

"Where are we going?"

"To my house."

I sniff my shoulder, my arm, my hair as we walk. But I don't smell lavender, or fresh cotton, or new-cut grass. I *do* smell fire—a whiff of smoke that curls from my skin to catch and twirl in the air.

Tom smells like cedar and honey and a forest path after a hard rain, and—

No, he doesn't. I am smelling Ebenezer.

Ebenezer. I slow and stop, watching the slope of the boy's shoulders, the sun glinting off his curls, his easy stride through the green glow of the glade.

Tom is here and not here. Or maybe he is most here, and I am the one who is here and not here.

The ground shifts, or maybe I shift.

A shadow flits above, covering me in darkness, and then passes on. I look up, and gasp. A dragonfly twice my size hums in midair and then lands on a nearby tree trunk. It settles its rust-colored wings and cleans its antennae, and I back away so fast I fall over, off the path into the water. It's only about a foot deep and warm, but still I shriek and flail.

Tom whips around and doubles over with a laugh. "What are you doing?" He offers his hand, which I take, slapping my slime-streaked palm into his.

"Dragonfly!" I say, gesturing with my free hand as he pulls me to my feet. "*Giant* dragonfly."

"Yes," he says. "Reliable when I need her, too. Come on." With a firm heft, he pulls me back to the path where I stand dripping, my head beneath his chin.

I yank my hand from his and bunch my sodden skirt around my knees as my wet ringlets of hair make streamlets down my shoulders. "Well, great," I say.

"It is, isn't it?" Tom says.

"No, not *really*."

Tom fixes his eyes on my face and says, "You don't *want* to be wet?"

"Of course not."

He touches my shoulder where the white strap of the dress rests on my skin, and the heavy skirt in my hands turns light and dry. I let it fall with a breathy exclamation.

"Then don't be," he says.

"I don't understand. I don't understand any of this."

"You're Queen," he says simply. "This is your Ebenezer now, too. Come on." He kicks his heel as he turns, sending dirt flying.

"Wait," I say, catching up to walk at his side. "Aren't you going to explain?"

"What do you want me to explain?"

"How about...the dragonfly."

"*The* Dragonfly." He looks back over his shoulder.

"That's what I said."

"Does she need explaining?"

"Of course she does! Dragonflies just don't get that big."

"Says who?"

"Says me, and, well, everyone."

"Everyone who? This is Ebenezer, and here it is just me and you. And here, I make the rules."

The ground shifts again. I tilt toward the edge of the path, and Tom tilts toward the other edge. Like magnets, we reach for each other, and our fingers meet in the center.

"*Do* you?" I whisper. "Make the rules?"

"I'm the king, the king of Ebenezer." He straightens, relaxes until our fingers fall apart. "This is my home, and here I stay. I make the rules of living, sleeping, eating, song, and play."

I suck my teeth and stare at him for a long time. "How did I get here?"

His face goes still as a stone, and then pinched, grey. The sky rumbles on the horizon with thunder. A storm, coming in from the East.

"Tom, *King Tom*. King Tom who makes all the rules—how did I come to your Ebenezer?"

"It's your Ebenezer now, too," he says.

"*Now*, but how—"

"Watch out!" Tom grabs my shoulders and spins me to face him, away from my edge of the path.

"What? What is it?" I look wildly around, but all I see are iridescent bubbles floating near the closest hanging vines.

As small as grapes, they pop and release from the surface of the water to travel lazily into the air in an irregular column. Sunlight filtering through catches them and sparkles off their perfect globes—they are floating crystals, filled with promises, filled with—

"Don't!" Tom snatches back my hand and presses it to my side. "Don't touch the floating bubbles."

"Oh…" I shake my head. I'd been reaching without thinking. "Wait, why?" I look up at Tom. He's holding me tight to his chest, so all I can see is his chin—the column of his neck. The honey and cedar scent floods me again, and I relax against him. Some force pulls my head toward his shoulder. It *wants* to rest there.

With a jolt, I step away. Tom keeps a light hand on my elbow but does not stop me.

"If you touch them, they will take you someplace else."

"Like outside Ebenezer?"

Tom tips his head and catches my eyes, and the amber light in his own eyes grows dim. "There is nothing outside Ebenezer," he says. "Ebenezer is all there is."

all there is

"What do you mean, Ebenezer is all there is?" I yank my elbow out of his grasp. "That's ridiculous. You *know* that's ridiculous. It can't possibly be true."

Tom's expression dims. "I know that can't possibly be true," he says, repeating my words back to me.

"Right...*right*."

"But it is," he says.

"I don't even know who you are!"

My hands shake as I cover my face to feel cold sweat beading my skin. What was, moments before, warm and lazy and magical, now feels fearsome. Clouds from the East roll in over the sun far above the leafy ceiling. "You said I just got here, but if here is all there is, then where did I come from?"

Tom puts his hands on his hips and paces away from me, down the path into a shadowy nook by a tall elm tree twisted in hairy, hoary vines. He stands akimbo and then turns back and says, "Where *did* you come from?"

"I came from—" I frown. Start again. Wipe the cold sweat from my cold brow in the cold shadows of the clouds. "Well, the...that is, I live..." But *where it is I live* recedes from me like a wave I can't catch on a steep shore, into mist, gone before I catch its form. "My island is back that way." I gesture to the last place I remember.

Maybe home is about remembrance.

Maybe Ebenezer is all there is.

No.

I lurch toward the column of rising, crystalline bubbles. "If I touch one of these, where will it take me?"

Tom pales and steps toward me, hand outstretched. A mist curls around us, a damp fog settling on the swamp.

"Where?" I say. "You said *someplace else*, but someplace else where? What are you afraid of?"

"I'm not afraid!"

"Yes, you are. You're terrified."

"I'm not!" he shouts, and the air cools even more. "But if you touch that, I might not be able to follow."

"And who made you my guardian?"

Tom slumps his shoulders. "Why do you want to leave?" he says. "Is it me? Am I not good enough for you to stay? Am I doing something wrong?"

He looks so forlorn I lower my voice to a whisper. "I'm trying to understand."

"My Ebenezer is perfect," he says. "Will you stay here with me?"

I touch a bubble.

Between one blink and the next I'm standing on the path, and then I'm lying on a forested floor in a bed of fallen leaves staring up at swaying boughs of elm and oak and longleaf pine. A misting rain starts to drizzle, cascading in dripping drops through to where I lie, gathering in my bunched hair and on my shoulders and face. I was cold already, but now I am freezing.

A shadow falls over me, and then a head the size of my torso—grey and angular with a beak large enough to swallow half my body. A crane, but no normal crane that I have ever known of...if I've ever known of cranes. This one is at least twelve feet tall with eyes as intelligent as a person's, and when he looks at me, his voice enters my mind.

"Going to lie in my bed all day, then? Or are you getting up? I know you're not dead. Dead things cannot here abide."

I shoot upright, gaping, gasping, grasping my shift. "I...am...lost—I mean, sorry! I didn't *expect*...anything, and certainly not that. Not *this*. You—you're—"

"Eli," he says.

"Okay. But you're a..." I don't have words for what he is. How do you tell someone he's a giant crane when that someone probably knows that already?

The bird, the, well, *Eli*, ruffles his feathers and walks a slow circle around me—plodding but silent, feet planting like splaying hands on the earth. He surveys me out of one beady eye and then the next. He seems curious, but not uncertain. I get to my feet and brush off my skirts, now dingy with damp leaves.

The slight rain continues to fall.

"Do you know why you are here?" Eli says, his voice again inside my head. His beak does not move.

"No," I say. "I don't even know where here is. I was hoping Tom would tell me."

"Ah." Eli completes his circuit. "And what does Tom say?"

"He said here is all there is." I swallow and give a quick look around at this clearing that no longer looks like a swamp. It's a forest, humid and still with air dense and hot and sort-of heavy. It is, I know without being told, still the place called Ebenezer. Tom's place. His kingdom.

"Is it true?" I wring my thick hair out of my eyes, peer

23

through the misting rain. "Is here really all there is?"

"What do you think?" Eli says.

"I think it can't possibly be true. *I* had to have come from someplace else."

"You only? Why? Why you and not Tom?" Eli tilts his beak.

"I don't know about Tom, but I'm new here. Even Tom says so."

"Where did you come from, then? And why are you here?"

Impatience rises in my chest. "*I* don't know. I can't remember how I got here, or what came before. I just know that Tom says I'm new here and, well, here I am!"

"Are you afraid?" Eli asks.

"No," I say. And somehow, it's true. I am not afraid— I am curious and impatient and lost.

"It would be understandable if you were. Most people are at first, in their own Ebenezers."

So, I'm not the first to experience...whatever this place is. And neither, apparently, is Tom. Buoyed, I ask, "Do *most people* know how they got here—or there, or wherever *this* is? Do people know where they, or we all, come from?"

The Crane lifts his ponderous head to the sky, as if sniffing, or petitioning someone for an answer he's hesitant to give. "You are asking the questions out of order," he says. He moves away into the forest, his great scaly feet pressing down foliage.

I scramble to follow. "Okay, then. What *is* Ebenezer? Can you tell me that?"

"Ebenezer is a place," Eli says. "A place for people like Tom. But not, I think, for people like you."

24

"What does that mean?"

"I am not yet sure. But I think we shall find out." He dips his head so one eye is next to mine. "Don't you?"

"If this place is for people like Tom, then who is Tom?"

"I should think you would know."

"Well, I don't."

"Tom is..." Eli sways his head this way and that. "Tom is as he says he is. Tom is the king of Ebenezer. Of *this* Ebenezer. A king of a sort, at least."

I sigh through my nose. "So he's told me."

"That is not answer enough for you."

"No."

"And yet, it will have to be."

"Why?" It's all I can do to keep from stomping my foot in frustration, like a child.

"Because, if you don't know who you are, and you don't already know who he is, how will you learn by asking me?"

We emerge onto a path—the same path, perhaps, that runs through the swamp? The rain and clouds clear and sunlight cuts through to the pine needle carpet. A mist rises from the hot earth, blanketing the open way with a thick, numinous veil. I warm, ashy smoke rising from my skin.

I smooth the wisps of dew and smoke from my honey skin and then look up at Eli. "I'm Beatrice, by the way," I say. "I'm sorry I didn't tell you my name. I do know that much, at least."

Eli inclines his head. "What bright eyes you have, child," he says.

"And I suppose I should go that way, to get back to

the swamp—where Tom is. Is that…my only option?" The trail winds away into the trees, into hushed green. The other direction, the sun is bright, bright like a portal. Too bright to wander into, it seems.

"Your options are before you," Eli says. "Your path will always be your own. Yes, even for you."

"What does that mean?"

Eli tilts his beak to the dew-woven air, and then says, "Ah."

A humming approaches, and then a large shadow descends, scattering the mist. The giant Dragonfly lands on the path and settles her wings—the humming ceases. Sitting casually astride it is Tom, one bare foot dangling, the other drawn up between the Dragonfly's wings. Across his back he carries the wooden staff with which he'd earlier bashed Ichabod the snake. He hops from his perch when the Dragonfly lands and swings the staff from his shoulders, planting it on the ground. He rests both hands on its end.

"Didn't go too far, then," he says, his voice light and carefree. His eyes are twinkling, but hidden inside is relief. "And you've met Eli."

"I suppose I have," I carefully say. "Who's this, then?" I'm certain the Dragonfly must also have a name.

Tom drops a casual glance over his shoulder. "Dinah."

"Dinah. Dinah the Dragonfly."

"Yes." He raises his chin looking pleased with himself.

"That's *really* her name?" I try to catch her eye, to see if she will talk with me as Eli has done. But dragonflies and cranes are not the same, and Tom's steed sits still, steady, and grave.

"What's wrong with that name? It's a good name."

"Nothing's wrong with it. It just seems...made up."

"All names are made up by someone at some time. It's up to us to get used to them."

"I suppose you're right." I quirk my lips. "You told the truth, about the bubbles."

"I tell the truth about everything in Ebenezer," Tom says.

"What about outside of Ebenezer?"

"Ebenezer is—"

"All there is," we say together.

"Yes," I whisper. "I understand," I lie.

"Should we go back to where we began?" Tom says. "I promise to try harder." He holds out his hand for mine, a crease between his eyes, wells of feeling that turn from amber to deep green.

I hesitate. A cloud skitters across the sky, plunging us all into shadow. Then I take his hand and my fingers fit in his. He smiles. The sky clears and the sun breaks through again.

"Should we walk, or should we ride?" Tom asks.

I study Dinah. Is this place impossible, or am I the impossible one?

"Ride," I say.

Tom grins from ear to ear. He helps me onto Dinah's back, shows me where to place my feet so they won't disturb her wings. He leaps nimbly on behind me and puts an arm loosely around my waist.

"So long, Eli," he says. "Are you ready, Bea?"

"Yes, I am. I'm ready!" I say, but my hands quiver and quake.

Dinah lifts us from the ground in a powerful slope of speed that sends me sliding backwards into Tom, and it's only once we're airborne that his words, his name, his name for me clamor back to the surface.

"Are you ready, Bea?"

Bea. *Bea.* My name—an endearment.

I've heard it before.

queen bea

I am Bea, and I am...*flying*—flying high above Ebenezer.

The trees stretch flat, left to right, horizon to horizon, a riot of green, interrupted only by glimmers of water. I glance over my shoulder to see the forest we left, the forest where Eli lives. Taller and darker trees, and on its far edge is a stretch of open land like a meadow leading to a wall, that wall of brightness that looked to me like the sun—but isn't. But Dinah turns and dips, and the openness is swallowed by green as the swamp embraces us.

On the horizon in the East is a rise of darkness—some high, dense place. Night has fallen there, twilight fingers reaching out toward Tom's home, my island, our home until...

The end?

I shudder. "What's over there?" I say, but Tom doesn't respond. I stare at the dark ridge until my eyes water, and when I blink, we are lower over the swamp, the waters, the green living place, and I cannot see the darkness anymore.

A swamp. But not a dirty, dingy swamp. A sparkling and mysterious one filled with life and transporting bubbles and nourishing honeysuckle and giant, talking animals. But it is, still, a swamp. Isn't it? *And swamps are dangerous.*

So, I ask what I think must be a practical question. "Are there alligators here?" I shout past the wind sliding down my throat. Shout this time, so Tom will be sure to hear me.

"Alligators? No. There's nothing in Ebenezer like *that*," Tom says. He sounds scandalized. "Nothing to break skin or bone."

I furrow my brow. "Bu—uuaa*aaaahh*..." A squeal swallows my question as Dinah banks over a dense spread of trees, descending in spirals that make me feel like I'm going to go flying off into the leafy canopy. Then she levels out, just above the tops of the uppermost trees, and hums on. With a shuddering breath, I say, "But what about Ichabod? He was, uh, trying to break my skin and bone."

"Ichabod? Nah. Ichabod does what I say."

"Yes, but. What if you aren't with me?"

"You're the queen of Ebenezer now. He won't hurt you."

"Yes, but, he *would* have hurt me. You said there's nothing like that here, and that you always tell the truth about Ebenezer. What is the truth?"

Against my back, Tom stiffens. Then he leans forward and whispers in my ear. "The truth is that Ichabod would never have hurt you. And here's another truth. If you catch Ichabod by the tail, he must tell you a secret. But only one secret. And he doesn't like being caught by the tail."

I shift to face him. "Is that how you became king of Ebenezer?"

Nose-to-nose, we stare until his eyes wash the darkest of greens, and then he says, "No," and looks away—down, and taps Dinah with a light finger. "Here," he says. "Here is close enough."

30

Dinah dives. I slam backwards into Tom, who laughs and goes taut for the dive. Then we are back on the path as near as like to where we first met, and Tom is getting off and offering me a hand that I don't take because I'm tumbling off into an ungainly heap.

"Bea—Bea, are you okay?" Tom says, taking me by the shoulders and setting me on my feet. He chuckles, brushes my curls out of my eyes. "Queen Bea, tell me you are okay?"

"I'm *fine*," I say. "Considering I've just flown on a dragonfly across a magic swamp."

Tom tilts his head like a dog that's caught a sound. "Magic?"

"Yes! Yes, *magic*. This is magic. All of this is magic." I sweep my arms in a wide circle. "The giant animals, the bubbles that took me far away, the—the honeysuckle."

Tom laughs and rocks back on his heels. "The what?"

"The honeysuckle," I say again, weakly. "Don't you know?"

"I don't, I guess. And I don't know about any *magic* either. What do you mean by it?"

I cross my arms. "What do *you* call it—all the stuff you can do here?"

Tom retrieves his staff from where he dropped it and taps it on the moist-packed earth. Blue butterflies erupt from where it lands—they flutter into the sky, as unbothered by their origin as the rain that falls from weighted clouds. "This?" he says.

"Yes, *that*."

"This isn't magic. This is being. It's living..." He struggles for a moment, bent over his staff. "It's truth."

31

My chest constricts. The butterflies are gone into the sky, but I am here, and I cannot fly away. I clutch the front of my gown in white-knuckled fists. "Is that how I...*became*? Did you do that to me?"

Tom's eyes cloud over. He steps to me—one step, two, until his breath warms my face. "You are true, but you are not like the rest."

"What does that mean, Tom?"

"It means I didn't bring you, I didn't name you, I didn't meet you, until today."

"I don't think *that's* true."

"It must be! I couldn't say it if it wasn't so."

"Well, maybe you believe it, but do you really think we just met?"

And then we stare at each other, and I'm besotted with memories I can't remember. And Tom clutches his throat and wanders from me, his eyes a-wonder. And after time we don't count, I say, "But...I am your queen?"

He blinks, coughs, nods. The swamp is hushed. Clouds like cotton skitter across the sky.

"Why am I your queen?"

"Because I know you." And again, he breathes freely.

I touch him, his chest, my hand presses there—palm flat against his beating heart. Where I know him, too.

Beats thump loud, like

knocks,

knocks,

knocks.

Tom makes a sound in his throat, of fear, so I wrap him in my arms and don't let go.

Because I am the queen of Ebenezer.

the second morning

I wake to the living earth, and Tom is sitting there.

His legs crossed, his brown feet bare and tucked in denim sleeves. On the earth, the place I first sprang into Ebenezer. My island.

I sit and swipe the sleep from my eyes. "Good morning," I say.

"Good morning." Tom wiggles his toes, smiles.

"Did you bring me here?" I press my hands to the earth, sit up, face him.

"I don't remember," he says. "But here we are."

"And it *is* morning?"

"As morning as it ever gets."

I laugh, because how can I not?

"This is my island, you hear?" I say. "My particular space." I stand and brush off my gown. "You can't just come here whenever you like. I have to have some privacy, if I'm stuck here."

"Oh." Tom's face clouds over. He stands, too, across from me. "I'm sorry. There's never been a place here before that I cannot go."

"It's okay." He looks so worried, his brow furrowed and his eyes dark and murky, that I take his hand in mine. "I don't mind that you're here today. But just so we're *clear*. For later."

"We are always clear," he says.

I wrinkle up my face. "Tom, I need to know more."

"I will tell you everything. All the truth of Ebenezer."

"Well, *good*, then."

He tightens our grip, and together we descend into the shallow water around my island. The way back to the path seems familiar now, and I walk side by side with Tom.

"We should look out for honeysuckle," I say.

"Why?" Tom's eyes flash in amusement as he glances at me.

"I'm hungry. Honeysuckle is food here, isn't it?"

"No." He raises an eyebrow. "Not that I've ever known. Unless you want it to be, of course."

"I don't understand."

"What did you mean by it?"

"I...well, I was hungry yesterday." I press my fingertips to my forehead, thinking back to the day before, trying to remember what exactly happened. "I was hungry for breakfast, and as I thought of it, I touched a tree and a vine with honeysuckle sprang to life on it. So I took some and ate it."

"Did it work?" he asks.

"You mean, did it fill me up?"

"Sure."

I nod, but I frown. Because it doesn't make sense. I haven't really been hungry since, but one honeysuckle shouldn't have stemmed my hunger for a morning, let alone a whole day. And... "It made me feel funny, too," I say.

"It's because you don't need to eat here," Tom says. "I never do. Not unless I want to—for the pleasure of it."

"Then"—I look up—"how do you know that food is a need, if Ebenezer is all there is?"

Tom's easy manner slides away as his shoulders

stiffen. A shadow passes over his eyes. "Come on," he says. "I'll show you where I live. You can stay with me—you don't have to go back to your island at all." He turns, tugging me to keep up with him.

"But I can't *stay* here. I have to find my way out. I have to go home. Eventually, that is—at the very least. Wherever home is."

Tom pauses, head bowed, back to me, his shoulders slumped. Then he drops my hand and plods on without a backward glance.

A misting rain begins to fall.

stay

I watch him go until he's almost disappeared into the greenery, and then, so I won't be alone, I follow.

He hasn't kidnapped me. At least, I don't think he has. He's too sad and funny and, well, *good* for that.

And Tom would never kidnap me. Tom would

never

never

never.

"Bea? Are you stuck?"

Tom is ahead, turned back to me, and his eyes are every bit as lost as mine. What if he is stuck, too?

"I'm coming," I say. I unstick my feet from the mud.

Tom would never kidnap me. We are in this together, like always. *Always.* I shake my head.

How am I to figure out where and what Ebenezer is when I am a mystery to myself?

We continue in staggered progression, and Tom climbs laboriously onto the path. He stands for a moment and then walks ahead, around a bend, until I can't see him. I hurry to the path as well and climb up, walk, dripping, forward to find...nothing. The swamp waters lap the sides, undisturbed, and tufts of long grasses tickle against each other in a gentle current.

"Tom?" I say. "Where'd you go?"

A whistle—from above. An acorn lands in my damp hair. I brush it off and tilt my chin to the canopy to see him sitting in the X of two crossing trees, at least twenty

36

feet in the air.

"How'd you get up there?" I search for a ladder or some hidden staircase, but there's nothing but greenery and the water all around.

"Take the leaves," he says. "They'll hold you if you believe."

"What leaves?"

"Those." He points to some swaying buttonbush, far too small and flimsy for a squirrel, let alone my weight.

I huff and lift my eyes back to him, incredulous.

He shifts so he's lounging along one crossed trunk, dangling an arm and resting his chin on his other wrist. Crossing his bare ankles, he looks like a jaguar, at home in his lofty domain. "Touch one," he says. "See what happens when you ask...*nicely*."

"And what am I asking for again?"

"To come up." He extends his dangling arm and wriggles his fingers, inviting.

With a laugh and a shake of my head, I approach a buttonbush frond. I don't know how I can ask it anything, but it does look like fun to join Tom in the tree...

My fingers brush the leaf, the white pom-pom dangling from it, and it shimmers and glows bright green and grows to three times its size.

"Oh!" I exclaim, leaping back.

"Not backwards," Tom says. "Forwards. Now, before it changes its mind."

"O-okay!" Half afraid the leaf will collapse under my weight and pitch me into the water, I spring onto it. But it holds.

"The swamp privet next," Tom says, pointing to a

weedy but bushy plant closer to him.

With a touch, it too shimmers and enlarges, and then I leap to land atop it. And the buttonbush shrinks back to normal.

"The creeper," Tom says. "And the alder."

My last leap takes me to the trunk of the tree and Tom's dangling arm, his hand reaching for me. He catches and pulls me up with ease to sit beside him. I'm exhilarated, beaming from ear to ear, heart pounding through my chest.

"You *are* my queen," Tom says, low and earnest, searching my face. He tucks a twirl of hair behind my ear. Then he matches my smile.

The sun has broken through again. Is the weather always this restless in Ebenezer?

I shift my gaze down, down to the swamp floor below. It looks like an Impressionist painting, yellow and white flowers planted flat on green leaves mixed with mud in eddying swirls.

"Why are we in this tree? I thought you were taking me to your home."

"I did. Look up."

Tom stands. He's as nimble on the tree trunks as I would have imagined him to be, but I quake as I get to my feet. Even after my miraculous ascent, my head whirls at the height, and I cling to Tom's hand to steady myself, wishing for guardrails.

But then I see. I see the house of green reeds perched above us at the far end of the crossed trees. The round opening in the round floor, and the vine hammock swaying off the side of it in the wind. I see Tom's house, and Tom ascending to it, my hand in his.

The tree trunk is not smooth or without marks to guide us but pegged with notches where Tom places his toes — as sure as a cat climbing a flight of stairs.

I go quickly with him. I have little choice, unless I want to release his hand and climb on my own (I don't). In moments, we reach his door, and he pushes through and pulls me after, and I find myself inside a cozy hut. Several bright green butterflies matching the color of the floor and walls take flight, disturbed by our sudden appearance, and flutter around me in a tight circle before flying out one of the four open windows. And then it's just me and Tom. I release him and tuck my knees to my chest and my skirt around my legs and gaze about the space.

A bed — just long enough for Tom, by the looks of it. Odds and ends hang from low rafters, and although the four windows let in streaming light this high in the canopy, pull-rods anchor shutters to the inside walls. Tom can shut those windows tight against weather.

I dart my eyes to him as he kicks a trapdoor closed over the entrance. There's a latch on the door, but he doesn't lock it. Outside one of the windows — the largest — swings the hammock I saw from below.

"Did you build this place?" I ask.

"Build it?" Tom turns, looking about his one-room abode as I just did — as though he's seeing it for the first time. "Yes. I suppose I did." He slaps a hand to a supporting beam over his head and swings himself to his bed, where he falls with a *whumpf.*

"It's nice."

"Thank you."

My stomach gurgles, loudly. As urgently as it did this

39

morning when I first woke up and Tom told me I didn't need to eat in Ebenezer. "Do you have any *food* here?" I glance around at his odds and ends.

Tom sits up, slowly, studying me with a frown. "You don't *need* to eat here."

"So *you* say." My stomach growls again. "But my body begs to differ."

His eyes flick down the length of me—back to my face. Then he slides from his bed and kneels by my side. "Place your hand on the floor," he says. "And think about your hunger."

"That won't be too difficult."

He takes my hand. "Do it." And he presses my palm to the reeds of his floor, adding his weight to my own.

"What are we doing?" I say.

"Ebenezer will provide everything you need," he says. "You just have to ask."

Between our fingers, a honeysuckle vine pushes up through the floor, parting the fibers with a creak and a crack, and an unfolding flower.

Tom lifts his hand and I lift mine, and I say with a laugh, "Honeysuckle again!" I pluck the flower, put it between my lips.

The green in Tom's hut pops, and it's so vibrant I gasp and reach for Tom to steady myself. But he's retreated to sit on the edge of his bed. He seems brighter now—brighter but pale. More present, but half-present, all at once. Sustenance rushes through me. I stand and brace myself against his wall. The sunlight coming through his window sparkles in waves off the humid air.

"Is that better?" Tom asks, and his voice is louder, inside my head. "Do you feel better?"

"I do." I stumble to his chair and sit, waiting for the rush to fade. Somewhere in the air, there is a beeping—too regular, too rhythmic. It doesn't belong here, in this hut, in this place. I grab my ears and shake my head, closing my eyes.

When I open them, I don't know how long it's been. But Tom still sits on his bed,

staring,

staring,

staring at me.

I lie back on the floor, until the world stops spinning.

When I come to, Tom is lying beside me, whistling.

"You don't need to eat here," he says again.

I raise myself onto my elbows and look down at him. "Well, what if *I* do?"

"What do you mean?"

"I mean, what if you don't need to eat here, but I do?"

"But you don't."

I sigh. "And how do you know?"

"Because there are no lies in Ebenezer."

"I thought that was just…" I struggle to put the words together. Now my *mind* wants to spin. "A you-thing. You always speak the truth in Ebenezer."

"Yes," he says. He frowns, touches the space between his eyes. "And yes."

With a huff, I flop back to the floor, lying beside him in a heap. Sun shines through the open windows, illuminating our toes, our feet—four standing statues in a row, mine inches shorter than his. Memory assaults me, of hot sticky days lying in long fragrant grass with

41

muddy toes in a row, wiggling while we giggled secrets in summer-kept ears.

A gasp. Mine. *A clutching*. My hands, on my chest, in my sweat-drenched gown.

"Tom."

"Yes?"

"Where are you from?"

"Here," he says.

I turn, capture his honey-green eyes in mine. "No, you're not."

His eyes darken,

darken,

darken.

"But here is where I'll stay."

the grey man

In one swift motion, Tom gets to his feet. "You can have the bed," he says. "I will take the hammock." He leans out the biggest window and sways it back and forth.

"I don't want the bed. I don't want to stay here at all."

"Why not?"

"Because, Tom..." I get to my feet as well, slower than him. I've been slower than him for a while. *Because.* This is fun for a visit, but I can't stay here with you—I barely know you!"

Tom stiffens and bends his face to the floor. His profile falls into shadow.

My tongue grows heavy in my mouth.

Tom's knees knock against the wall. Then he climbs onto the window ledge and sits, legs dangling.

Two long strides and I'm at his side. I touch his neck, his grey and ashy skin. He warms under my featherlight fingers. "Are you sick, Tom?" I ask.

"There's no sickness in Ebenezer," he says.

I don't believe him, but I don't believe I should say so.

"Then why are you sad?"

Tom pushes off of the edge of his window and drops into the sea of green below.

"Wait, no!" I grab the windowsill in time to see him running—running away down the path. His feet kick leaves, and puddles, as rain falls, soft at first, but then quick and hard. So, Tom can *jump*, and land, at need.

I retreat into his house and listen to the drops against the thatched roof. There are voices in the rain. If I close my eyes, I can almost hear what they say.

There are voices *out there*, too. Voices everywhere. Not animals. *People*. And metal, and fear, and a

howl,

howl,

howl...

I open my eyes to the owl.

It sits in Tom's window, staring at me, ordinary size, but so many eyes. It blinks one eye, six at once, then three, but it never stops looking.

"So, who are you, then?" I say, wondering what name Tom gave this beast. And if it talks like Eli or is silent like all the rest.

"I am Minerva," says the Owl.

Minerva. Her voice is all around, not inside my head like Eli's was. It's on the air, quiet, but loud as thunder, and I wonder if the whole swamp can hear her speak.

"Why are you here?"

"Because you are here."

"Not—not for him?" I glance beyond her, out the window, out to where we both (must) know Tom has run away into the trees.

"I am here for you, and you are here for him, we think." She ruffles her feathers.

Above, the rain keeps falling. Torrential waves of it.

I stare into Minerva's many eyes. Below, on the path, something comes. It knocks on trees as it passes.

Knock,

knock,

knock.

And silence. And then closer.

Knock,

knock,

knock.

The air cools and my breath rushes out of me on a cold, moisty coil. And the rain transforms to snow.

Knock,

knock,

knock.

Beneath Tom's house, it waits.

I won't let it in! I won't! I squeeze my eyes shut and curl over my knees.

A flutter of tawny feathers. Minerva rests on my back, covering me with her wings.

"Don't be afraid," she says. "The Grey Man is not here for you." Her voice, this time, is inside my head. "But you, I think, will come for him."

the wish

This time, I wake up with a scream. I don't know if time works differently here in Ebenezer or if this is how time always works, but I have once again fallen asleep on my island and awoken the next day.

I don't know how I got here, back to this spit of land I call my own.

I am hungry, but I will not eat. I will keep my head clear and trust what Tom has said, that I do not need to eat in Ebenezer.

Because now, I do not trust the honeysuckle.

A scream. My scream. A storm that raged, the cold, snow. No. A Grey Man who knocked...he knocked for me. *No, for he. Him*. For Tom.

Minerva told me so.

I push myself up from the soft earth, away from the fairy ring. I splash into the water and

stomp,

stomp,

stomp

to find him.

This is now the third day, I think at least. *And I need to know*. The day is bright and sunny, and Ebenezer is alive with animal sounds. I splash from tree to tree, my toes dig deep in the mud until the water climbs to my knees. Dragonflies, the ordinary kind, investigate. Land on shoulders, in my hair. Fly away.

"Tom! Where are you?"

Only birds answer.

I should go to the path and carry on, look for him the way he walked yesterday, when he ran away from me. But the wild uncharted water feels safer than the trodden path—today, after the dark and cold of yesterday, when the Grey Man came.

I shiver and glance at the sky, expect the cold to fall again. Yet, only green leaves wave back at me. Warmth coils off the surface of the swamp, off my skin and my gown, floating in a halo around me. Water bugs dance and skate, just beyond my wake.

Ichabod could be anywhere. But Tom said if I catch him by the tail, he has to tell me a secret.

Maybe I should be *looking* for Ichabod to tell me the secret of this place.

To tell me how to get home. Wherever home might be.

Because I think home must feel different than this.

Bubbles, in a column, rise near to my face.

"Tom?" I shout again.

Laughter rises in the air. He's near, somewhere. Playing with me.

"Ooh, Tom, if you won't *come* out, then I will *go* out."

"Where?" he says.

I turn and look. The water makes a green swirl around my knees. "Anywhere I want. I'm the queen of Ebenezer, aren't I?"

He laughs again, an invisible ovation that rustles the trees and sets the rushes to dancing.

"Come and swim with me," he says.

"I will not *swim* in a *swamp*."

"Why not?"

"Because it is a swamp and that is a ridiculous thing to do!"

"But you are walking in a swamp."

I tut and fold my arms.

And then a hum and a shadow, and my feet leave the mud and my skirt sucks and pulls me down as I lift into the balmy sunny air. I swallow a shriek as Dinah's legs pincer me, carry me, swoop me—feet, yards, through the trees to a deeper part of the swamp. I brace, expecting Dinah to drop me into water that might, must, cover my head, but she places me like a gentle thing on a warm patch of ground at the edge of the water, and she buzzes away like she didn't just obey the whims of a forest *child*.

I sit up, steaming. I look around.

This is the path, again. The end of the path, maybe, because from here there is nothing more than a wall of trees. Or maybe this is *one* end to the path, and there are infinite bends and branches I yet know nothing about.

How far does Ebenezer go? How big is it—and how might I get to the dark forest on the ridge that I saw from the air?

A splash. Tom paddles by, floating on his back and stroking his arms in lazy half-circles, face turned to the sun, jeans and white t-shirt a second skin. "Are you sure you won't swim with me?" he says. He peeks open one eye; it twinkles at me like a star.

I pull my knees up inside my sodden skirt and hug myself. "Why do you want me to? Will you have Dinah dump me in the water if I continue to say no?"

"Of course not. You are free to do what you want."

It's my turn to laugh. "Except leave."

A cloud skitters across Tom's face. He jackknifes, disappearing into the water in a burst of bubbles.

I lean over the edge of the path, stretching out. "Tom?"

He reappears suddenly, before me, holding something in his hand. "Here," he says, and touches my fingers. "Take it."

"What is it?"

He comes closer, water droplets glistening on his lashes, his cheeks, his lips. "A wish," he says. "A wish for you."

He's warm and flush today, no sign of the ashiness of yesterday. His elfin eyes bore into mine with all the promise of every day and every memory we hold together. *I wish I could remember.*

Tom presses his wish into my hand, and I curl my fingers around it.

"It's a rock." Smooth and undescriptive, a river rock from the bed of the swamp. A bare and boring stone. I breathe a laugh and hold it up between us. "A rock, Tom."

"It's a wish if I say it's a wish." A fierce light enters his eyes. "I am the king of Ebenezer."

"Okay, Your Majesty."

I move to set it on the path, but Tom jerks his chin wildly side-to-side. "Don't lose it."

"Okay, Tom. I won't." I tie the wish into the hem of my gown, tie it tight, where it hangs heavy against my leg.

Tom pushes far from the bank, parts the water rushes and swamp lilies. "Come swimming with me, Bea," he says. "Like we used to."

49

Clouds have rolled in, and the air has cooled.
But I am on fire.
I close my eyes and jump.

a secret

We swim for a long time, far into the day. I wonder if it's my first *afternoon* here, but I don't really know. I've stopped trying to keep track of hours, of minutes, of seconds that don't make sense. The third day, but the first time I can recall an afternoon, perhaps. I am living, but not wakeful. Here, but not.

And also, swimming. We talk about silly things, imitate animal calls, and splash water into each other's faces. We float and chew on cattails and stare at the re-emerged sunlight as it drifts through the green canopy. And when we drag ourselves up to the path, we don't bother to dry, but lie flat like starfish, absorbing the day.

"What if," I say, draping my dripping hair over my eyes. "I walk and walk and never stop. What then?"

"Walk where?" he says with a laugh. "And why?" Tom parts the curtain I made over my eyes, wrinkles his funny lips into a goofy smile.

"Exactly!"

He returns the wet strands of hair to cover my eyes and flops to lie next to me on the damp but drying earth. "Nothing. Nothing then. You cannot simply walk out of Ebenezer. And…"

"Yes?" I puff, huff, freeing my face.

"There are some places you would not want to walk." He says it quickly, in a rush, as though ashamed.

"Here—in Ebenezer?" I rise onto my elbow and look down at him. At the dewy drops of water on his skin, at the still-transparent patches where his white shirt clings to his chest, rising and falling. At how he sprawls, long legs and arms, tossed.

I blink.

"Tom."

He blinks. The clouds blink. The earth shudders.

"*A* place you would not want to walk," he says. "We do not go there."

In the trees beyond us, the great shadow of Eli meanders by, pauses to dip his head to the water. Moves on.

I follow Eli's movement until he disappears into the recesses of the swamp, and then I say, "But I thought you control everything that happens in Ebenezer, or something like that. Don't you *know it all*, at least?"

He looks at me and quickly looks away.

"You lied to me!"

"I did not." He sits. "I cannot." He crosses his legs like a child. "I do know it all—but not you."

"And not him—not the Grey Man that came—"

Tom springs up, suddenly dry, and there is escape in his eyes. But I grab his pants cuff, cling and hold.

"Let go!" He shakes his foot.

"I won't, not until you tell me the truth!"

"I always tell the truth."

"Then…tell me a secret. Tell me a secret I need to know." I wrap myself around his feet, curl up like a cat so he cannot leave.

He becomes still like the air, like a tree in the swamp. "Sometimes I want the Grey Man to find me," he says. "And that scares me more than the Grey Man himself."

I let him go. I am dry now, too, and my hair bounces

in golden ringlets around my face. "I won't let that happen. I won't let him find you."

Tom sits cross-legged again, across from me. He waggles his finger in front of my eyes. "There is no lying in Ebenezer."

"I am not lying!"

Tom crumples over himself, folding like paper, face in his hands. His sobs wake the swamp, which pours forth creatures to comfort him. Turtles and snails climb out of the muck to bump against his legs, birds flutter down from the trees to peck and pick at his hair and shirt, rabbits hop to his side, and squirrels and chipmunks—two perch right on his knee. Archibald and Shiloh, I can only assume. Fish leap in silver arcs out of the water. A pair of beavers waddle forward and deposit chewed limbs around us, making a fence, a hedge.

I grasp his hands, pries his fingers apart. I touch his cheeks and wipe his tears away, and I feel the truth of what I said. I was not lying. *I* will protect him from the Grey Man. Me. It is what I will do.

Tom is right that there is no lying in Ebenezer, and I am coming to understand Tom, even if I don't know where we are or what we're doing here, or even who we are. Somehow

I do,

I do,

I do

believe him. And, in my heart—the only thing unenchanted in this enchanted place—I love him.

I love him.

I am no prisoner of Ebenezer; I am a guest. And that means I can leave whenever I want.

But Tom.

There is a flutter of wings overhead, and Minerva
alights on a nearby limb. All her eyes are bright and

    staring,

    staring,

    staring

    at me.

night falls

Night falls in Ebenezer like night in any other place.

Not that I can remember any other place.

But some part of me must remember because I know that night falls in Ebenezer like night in any other place.

Dusk comes first, creeping through the swamp, hushing the birds and the creatures that huddle and hurry and scurry along the path ahead of us. Night follows on the heels of dusk, folding over us like a blanket. We walk, hand-in-hand, returning to places I am more familiar with, stepping into night-cloaked haunts. The path branches, but the path that leads off goes away into darker, closer trees, and Tom averts his eyes and hurries past.

We return to where the water is shallower, and the trees aren't so dense. There is a song of night here when the world goes dim and quiet. Darkness brings lights in the sky. Ebenezer is bright, even at night. Voices hum about us, calling back and forth words I cannot comprehend.

"Do you remember," I say, and then I stop. Because I can't remember.

We carry on.

At his treehouse, at the base, he says goodnight. And we linger, and away in the distance, three knocks sound.

He looks East, and I look up. "I think I'll stay here," I say. "If the offer still stands."

"I wish you would."

We ascend together, the leaves quivering under our weight, until we're through and into the green house high above the path below. Tom shutters each window and we are plunged into darkness.

But then the darkness isn't dark because I can see, as long as Tom is near me. He settles onto the floor— stretches out near the bed and props both hands behind his head. A gentle sound pulses through the hut, like a heartbeat. I lie on the feathered fronds of Tom's bed, settle onto soft greenery, look over the edge, at him.

"Where will you sleep?" I say. "It's not safe for either of us out there, in the hammock, is it?"

He shakes his head, eyes wide like marbles, like planets, like stars in the night sky. "I'll sleep here on the floor, if that's alright with you."

"It's your house. You can have the bed, if you like, and I will take the floor."

"No, Bea. The floor is no place for a queen."

I smile. "No place for a king, either."

"Maybe it's the only place for me."

"Why don't you just make yourself another bed? You made this whole house, didn't you?"

Tom shifts and lifts his hands. "I can't create when he is near," he says.

I lean over the edge of the bed, my chin hovers over knuckles taut and white. "The Grey Man. You can't create when he is near?"

He shakes his head. He lies stiff, like a board, like a corpse on the floor.

"Tom. If *we* are the only two people in Ebenezer, then who is—*what* is—"

Tom skitters his eyes at me, and quick as a mouse,

he scurries under the bed. "We don't talk about him," he says.

I hang my head to look upside down at him, curled up in the shadows beneath me. "I think we ought to. How will I know how to protect you if I don't learn more about him?"

"*We don't talk about him.*"

"But we *have to* talk about him. And we have mentioned him before—I just need to know more!"

Tom explodes out from under the bed, rocking it up on two legs and sending me tumbling to the floor. "*WE DON'T TALK ABOUT HIM!*" he shouts. "Not when he's hunting, Bea!"

Outside, the sky erupts in thunder and lightning, and the shutters of the largest window burst open, splattering us with cold, wet rain.

Knock,

knock,

knock.

I clamber to my feet, stumble toward the window, but Tom grabs my arm and pulls me back.

"No!" he says, pressing me to his side. "There's no time—we have to hide!" He drags me to the wall to where the bed has gone on end. The wind blows and blows, drenching us, and we crouch behind the furniture where the wind can't reach us and the dark is almost complete.

Knock,

knock,

KNOCK.

He's right beneath us now.

I throw my arms around Tom, feel his shaking bones. I want to tell him to imagine a place far away from

57

here, where it is warm and dry and safe and bright, but I can't remember any place like that—not now with the Grey Man at our door. So instead I hum a quiet song as soft as can be, and the trees around us hum it back at me. The pulsing center of the house, perhaps of Ebenezer itself,

beats,

beats,

beats,

and a voice says, "He's stable now," and that voice is not mine.

And the next three knocks are far away.

The song of Ebenezer continues…

Long after I stop singing.

He falls asleep first, slumped over in my lap, arms relaxing from a desperate life-grip on my waist to loll at my sides. His honeyed cedar scent returns, it fills the house, the space, the swamp. It fills, perhaps, the universe itself. A warm breeze chases away the chill of the Grey Man, and heat rises from the floor. I lie back, careful not to disturb the king, wishing the floor to be softer than it is.

And then—it is. It's soft like a leaf, floating on water. Soft like moss under a tree. Soft like starlight.

Maybe the floor is the perfect bed for a king and a queen after all.

I'm tired, and for the first time since I came here, I know that I am falling asleep.

honey and bees

Tom wakes first. I know this because when I wake, he's already sitting and staring at me, arms on his knees and head tilted like a puzzled bird.

"You're still here," he says.

"Of course I am."

"I thought you would be afraid. I thought you would leave."

"I'm not afraid of him, and I said I would protect you."

Tom swallows so his throat bobs, so tears gather in his eyes. He looks away, toward the open window that streams dim sunlight in a straight beam onto the wall. "Not afraid of him. Afraid of me."

"How could I ever be afraid of you?" I draw myself up to sit in the light.

"I shouted last night."

"Because you were scared."

"I hid, I tossed the bed."

"You did." I can only tell the truth in Ebenezer. I smile to let him know it's okay—okay to be afraid. But telling the truth also means that I meant what I said: I am not afraid of the Grey Man.

"What should we do today?" I say. "Should we go swimming again?"

"No."

"Is there more to explore? Surely you haven't shown

me all there is."

"I don't know."

"Yes, you do. You know everything that goes on in Ebenezer."

He trails his eyes to the floor.

"Come on, Tom. Come and walk with me, at least."

"Time, time, time," he says, under his breath, a susurration.

"What does that mean?"

"There is no time."

"No time for a walk?"

"There's no time for anything. He will find me, in the end. What's the point?"

The light isn't light anymore, so I get up and open the remaining shutters, poke my head outside and look around. Day has turned to night again. Did we sleep the whole day through? Or is this...

Tom is covering his face, his eyes, shuddering from head to toe.

"Tom, stop it," I say. "Stop it right now."

"I don't know how to stop," he says, his voice sounds far away.

"Just, breathe. One breath in, and another breath out. Breathing is as easy as letting yourself be, isn't it?"

"Isn't it?" he says. He echoes me like a person drifting from shore. Farther he drifts. Farther.

I return to him, kneel at his side. "Tom," I whisper in his ear. "We are thick as thieves. We are honey and bees. We are you and me. Come back, Tom. Come back and be. Come back to me."

His head thunks against the wall. His eyes open and he stares, un-shuddered. The sunlight comes, and he touches my cheek. "I remember you," he says. "You are the queen of Ebenezer."

I smile, I kiss his fingertips with the familiarity of friendship. "*Now* can we take a walk?"

"Why walk when we could fly?" he says, and the elfin smile twitches against the corners of his mouth.

It's a smile that has always made me jump.

And Dinah is there, outside the window waiting for us, as quick as Tom's thought.

"Where are we going?" I say. I get on behind Tom this time and wrap my arms around his waist, press my face between his shoulder blades, lock my hands tight to their old familiar place.

"Wherever you want," he says. "You're the—"

"Queen of Ebenezer."

Queen,

Queen,

Queen

of a kingdom?

I cough. I choke on ash, on smoke.

"Where are we going?" I say again. This time, my voice cracks and trembles.

This time, Tom says nothing at all.

are we dead?

This sameness—can't go on forever. Without food or drink, without real passage of time. We don't need to eat, so do we even *need* to sleep? Tom tires and sleeps, but I just sleep. And wake. And sleep again.

I lost track of days a long time ago.

We explore every corner of Ebenezer, every vine and tree, every current and stream. All but two: the bright meadow beyond where Eli sleeps, and the dark ridge where I assume the Grey Man lives.

The Grey Man, who comes almost every day, or night, or any time between. Knocking on trees—he hasn't found us yet.

I haven't changed my clothes and I don't know why. Tom told me I could wear anything I want in Ebenezer, and I believe him. But my nightgown clings to me like a second skin, like something real here where nothing is. Or where everything is inside, and the nightgown is outside. I don't know how to describe it, but I can't bring myself to change. Tom doesn't change either.

I lost track of days a long time ago.

I finally ask Tom the question most pressing on my mind:

"Tom, are we dead?"

He rolls over, looks at me with eyes as deep as the water at the edge of the path—that is to say, not very deep. He's in a laughing mood—mirthful, chasing clouds across the sky with chest-deep chuckles.

"*Dead?*" He twiddles with the hem of my gown.

"What are you talking about?"

"Well, if we aren't dead, then I don't know what we are!"

"We are…" He frowns, he sits. "Alive. Don't you feel alive?"

"I don't know. The longer I spend here, the more I worry that I've forgotten what alive feels like. Or that maybe I haven't known it since I got here." Smoke curls off my skin—I brush it away, impatiently.

"Don't be ridiculous, Beatrice." Tom draws his knees to his chest, curling in on himself like a shriveling leaf. Like a pill bug pulled from the earth.

"What is ridiculous about that question? Do you think this is normal? Are we just going to go on like this forever? Because if this is forever, then we must be dead!"

"We are not dead. Dead things cannot here abide."

A memory piques as clouds gather over Tom's brow, over us. "Those aren't your words," I say.

"I didn't steal them!"

"No, but I've heard them before. That's what Eli told me back when…when I first got here." Eli, who I haven't seen in a long time. "I want to see him again."

"Who, Eli?"

"Yes." I get to my feet. "I think I will go. Come along if you wish."

Tom leaps up beside me. "Why do you want to see Eli? What can he tell you that I cannot?"

"Everything, maybe. Or nothing at all. What does it matter, if nothing ever changes?" I walk away, away from our pond where we swim sometimes, away from the leaping silver fish who visit us. Tom scrambles to keep up. He may run from me, but he does not like to be left alone.

"Day after day, it's all the same. Same path, same trees, same friends," I say. Shiloh and Archibald keep pace at my feet—out in the eddying water, Ichabod weaves a curving S. I feel his eyes on me. "The same!"

"Sameness doesn't equal death," Tom says, digging his hands into his pockets. He kicks dirt down the path ahead of us. "Sometimes sameness is just...*staying*."

"Staying. Staying where?"

"*Here*." He stops, all of a sudden. He breathes so hard his chest raises and lowers the hem of his plain white shirt. "Bea. *Bea*."

"What is it, Tom?"

"Stay with me."

We grasp hands, faces, kiss on the lips. We've done this before.

"We can't *stay* here, Tom." I say the words on tiptoe, my breath against his ear. "We have to run away."

Run away. *Run away with me.*

Smoke curls off my skin, out of my hair. Tom coughs and his knees go weak against mine. The ground beneath us shifts, tossing us both to the side where we lie in a heap.

I crawl from under Tom to the column of bubbles rising off the path. I hold tight to his hand, and then—

the meadow

Light as bright as the sun. I can't see my hand in front of my face, but I know Tom is still with me; I hold him as tight as the earth holds the moon. We are in orbit.

"What did you do?" he says. "What did you *do*? Where did you take us?"

"I think we're..." I shade my eyes—pointless. "That place," I say. "The place with the bright wall, near where Eli sleeps."

"There is no such place," Tom says. He sounds fearful.

"Yes, there is! Beyond the forest, there's a meadow, and—"

"Are we *in* the meadow?"

"I guess we must be!"

The light, if we turn inward to Ebenezer's swamp, is dimmer, and I can see a little. Tom grows sharp before me, his face arrested in the light, his back in shadow. Trees rise like wolves' teeth beyond a long stretch of the greenest grass.

But Tom's skin is grey with pallor, his eyes wide and dark, reflecting no light. "We shouldn't be here," he says. "This is the edge of Ebenezer."

"You said Ebenezer was all there was."

"It is all there is. There's nothing there."

I gesture, a wide arc with my free hand. "It's light— it's warm! Maybe we should press on, Tom. Walk through it and see what's on the other side."

"It's not warm or light or anything at all," he says. "There's *nothing*. It's a void. You would ask me to step into a void?"

"I..." It's not a void, is it? Ahead, the wall pulses with light—light that beats and beeps, rhythmic with a song not of this place. "You can't see it?"

He wrenches his hand from mine, backs away toward the teeth, the trees, the forest that surrounds Ebenezer's swamp. "I can't go that way. There is no light."

I take a step away from Tom, toward the pulsing light and life. I take another. "I could, if I wanted to."

Tom stumbles and sits, hard, in the grass. He crosses his legs and stares at nothing, the nothing he sees.

No thing, no light reflected in his eyes. His face as grey as death, but we aren't dead. We can't be. *Dead things cannot here abide.*

"*Tom*," I say, as loud as I can without shouting, without screaming, without frightening him more than he already is. "If you cannot see the light, at least choose me. Run away with me!"

In the East, the far ridge rumbles and rain falls in a sheet that sweeps the sky away. A shadow of a man as big as a mountain rises and steps over the swamp; in three great strides, he'll be upon us. I throw myself at Tom, but the earth tilts until I'm falling—falling toward that bright, white light. The nothing—the no thing that he can't see.

"No—Tom!" I reach with both hands to him, to Tom who is pinned to the earth like a bug to a board, crossed legs like butterfly wings, spread arms to embrace—

66

Me.

I slam into him. I don't know how. One second, falling away. The next, we're together, as we should be.

I smell salt. Tears. A chord of struck iron runs through my skull.

In another stride, he will be here. The Grey Man comes.

"Help us," I say to the wildly tilting world.

"Help us," says Tom. "Hide us."

The earth shakes, and Eli is here, shadowing us with his wings.

Like a mother hen, he gathers us, and in a rush of cold wind and salt spray, the Grey Man passes.

We huddle under Eli together, breathing into the soft and downy feathers on the underside of his wings. Tom shudders, shudders again, jolts, and lies still. I press my hand to his chest, but he's electric, on fire, steaming with heat.

"Tom?" I try again, and he's cooler now, cooling like a hot iron plunged into a bath.

A breath—his breath, shuddering against my cheek.

"He doesn't like it when I come to the meadow," Tom says.

"I understand. I see that now."

"I cannot come to the meadow—when I come here, he sees me."

"I'm sorry, Tom. I didn't know what would happen. But he's gone. He didn't find you."

"He's gone *now*. He will be back."

"But not...today?"

Tom turns his face to mine, and there is something glimmering in his eyes. Tears? No. It is the reflection of my own eyes, bright like stars in the shadow of Eli's wings.

"No, not today, I don't think," he says. "Not if Dinah takes us back."

"Back to the swamp."

He lowers his gaze, and the light disappears.

"How many days has it been? How long before I came?"

"I don't know," he says. He curls on his side, away from me. "It's always been."

Above us, Eli shifts so a sliver of the bright white from the edge of Ebenezer slips into our refuge. I curl around Tom and hold on.

a killer

That night, I go back to my island. I leave Tom asleep in his house and return to my own, my special place that I have mostly abandoned to watch over this forest boy who is as dear to me as my own body and breath. More, even, and I can't explain why.

The fairy ring greets me with flowers unfolding to the moon and verdant grass, the ground pliable to my pressing knees. I kneel and search—search for a clue, any clue. This is either where I entered Ebenezer or simply the first place I remember. If there was anything before this, I will find the answer here.

But I find nothing. There are no answers as there is no time as we need no food or sleep as I feel no fear. Except for when he is in danger. Then I shake with the earth itself.

Tom is right—we are not dead, for if we were dead, I think there would be no danger and we would not ever be afraid.

I stretch out and breathe in the earth, breathe out my hot frustration. Breathe in, roll over, look up at the moon. It's full. It's always full in Ebenezer, as if to be at its brightest so that night is never too dark. Minerva swoops overhead, a crescent silhouette against the bright sky. She watches me still with her many eyes, never sleeping.

"What do you want from me?" I say.

Nothing and nobody answers.

No answers.

But I can leave, if I want. On the horizon, the bright veil beyond the meadow illuminates the canopy of the swamp—but not the sky. If I were to take the path all the way back to the forest, I could find where Eli makes his abode. And beyond that, the meadow. Beyond that the place where I could walk out of here. But Tom was right—not *simply* walk. There is nothing simple about it.

I am certain, now.

As certain as I am that Tom will not come with me that way without some great struggle or release or permission to go. Maybe he cannot. He is tied here, by some means I can't decipher.

On the opposite horizon, the canopy is swallowed in the darkness of the ridge, as dark as its mirror is bright. If I were to go that way, I'm not sure what would happen. Maybe it is another way out.

Between the two edges of Ebenezer, we wait. But I don't think we can wait forever.

So, maybe I must go to the ridge to save the boy I love. Tom wouldn't let me, if he knew. And he won't like it when he finds out. But Minerva said I would come for him, the Grey Man. And how can I come for him if I do not go?

I sit up in a rush before my resolve can flee, and the whispers on the wind of the swamp air grow dim, as if waiting for me to speak.

"I will go," I say. "And I will find the Grey Man."

"And what will you do when you find him?" Minerva says, fluttering down to land on a limb hanging low over the water.

"Whatever I must do to set Tom free."

"What if the Grey Man is not his jailor?"

"Isn't fear its own sort of prison?"

Minerva ruffles her feathers. "What makes you think Ebenezer is a prison?" She launches into the night air. "Or that Tom cannot leave it," she says in a voice none the fainter for the growing distance between us.

I scramble from my perch on my island, splashing into the water, making a mess of myself. "What if...what if I kill the Grey Man to save my friend?" The question falls hard and sudden from my lips—as hard as it's been weighing on my chest. "He may not be a jailor, but he's certainly a threat. And you said I would come for him!"

"Are you a killer, Beatrice?" Minerva asks, her voice soft inside my head.

I do not know. I do not know what I am.

I know only that I love my friend.

i leave

I revisit the house—Tom's house—before I go. Leaping up the plants as light as a bird, the magic of the place second nature to me now. In through the trap door, across the floor to Tom's sleeping form. He sleeps like one enchanted, deep and sprawled with limbs splayed, chest barely moving. I drop a kiss on his cheek, inhale cedar and honey, promise, "I will be back," press the promise into his mind and will for it to stay.

To the window, I leap out, down, down to the forest floor below. Tom's trick is my trick now. I am the queen of Ebenezer and I move here like he does.

They watch me go—Ichabod and Shiloh and Archibald. Quiet companions, pace-keepers, judging eyes. When I get to where the path branches into shadows, the mouse and the squirrel turn back and run away, but Ichabod hisses and snaps.

And then he speaks. "You cannot kill him, idiot girl."

I pivot on one heel stuck firmly in the dirt of the path to the East, my way set. Somehow, I am not surprised that Ichabod can speak. "You were spying on me on my island," I say. "And eavesdropping."

"Don't you know who he is?"

I exchange a long, cold stare with the long, cold snake. "If I knew, I wouldn't go and see him. Is that what you're getting at?"

Ichabod bunches himself into a knot against the

roots of an old elm tree. "You will accomplish nothing, and Tom will wake up alone."

"He was alone before I got here."

"That was different."

"Why?"

"He didn't understand his aloneness. Now that he does, to be alone in this place will be the ruin of him—it could bring the Grey Man right to his door."

I stomp my foot on the hard earth. "That's why I'm going! We can't live—we can't *stay here*, always, with this threat of the Grey Man over our heads. One of us has to do something about it, and if Tom can't, then I must."

Ichabod hisses. Away in the East, the dark ridge rumbles.

"If you're so worried about him waking up alone, why don't you go and be with him? You and Shiloh and Archibald and all the other creatures of this place? Everyone here who loves and cares about him. Surround him until I get back."

"We will," says Ichabod, "but it won't make any difference. We are of Ebenezer, you are in it. When we are with Tom, he is still alone. And now he understands."

I leave the branching path, kneel by Ichabod. "Who is the Grey Man? Tell me this secret. How do I defeat him? Maybe, being...*different* from the rest of you, I am the only one who can." My fingers twitch, and with a darting grasp I grab him by his tail.

Ichabod's scales constrict in my hand, and I let go as fast as I took hold.

"You already claimed your secret, Queen," he says. "Though you did not realize it at the time. And it is not a great secret who the Grey Man is." Ichabod flickers his tongue, tasting the air between us. "I will not tell you something you should know already and will shortly determine if not. But I will tell you that you cannot defeat him—you can only draw his eye. Go back to Tom and leave well enough alone."

"*You* go to Tom." I stand, I raise my chin to the darkness. "Tell him I have not abandoned him—that I am coming back. But I have no choice but to take this path—to go and find out for myself how to save him from the Grey Man."

"If you take that path, all you will find is pain and fear," Ichabod says.

But when I twist to glance back at him, he's gone.

into darkness

Buzzing insects are the first thing I notice. In the swamp, there are no buzzing insects. There are dragonflies and butterflies and water bugs that skip and race across the surface of the swamp, but nothing buzzing, biting, or tickling. Nothing that needs swiping or swatting. But as I walk this path, away from the swamp trees and into forest trees unlike the pleasant forest where Eli lives, a hum of insect noises descends.

I slap my arms and remember...

Hot sticky nights, his hand in mine. Running through fields of grass, blades soft against bare feet. Sharp mosquito bites on hot sticky skin. Laughter.

I'm not laughing now.

Slap, another bug burrowing into my skin. The trees are dense and tight, so tight the bright full moon doesn't shine here. But my gown glimmers white, casting a glow across the path, across my toes that push through pine needles. A spider scurries across the edge of my halo of light.

A feeling catches in my chest, heavy and cold, and I stop, fight the urge to turn back. It's more than fear, it's terror. I am terrified of spiders, but I don't think I always have been. It's a terror that is leaking through the seams of this world. *A sympathetic horror*.

He hates spiders—Tom does. I remember, one time, a spider caught in his shirt—how it ran from his collar down his sleeve and dropped from frozen fingers to the ground on a silver thread. How Tom shrieked and ran.

How I ran after him, laughter buttoned behind a forced frown. Spiders were never funny to Tom.

I take another step and another. Keep moving until the voices of Ebenezer fall silent and all I hear is the buzzing of insects and the creaking of tall trees swaying overhead and my own heartbeat loud in my ears.

Sooner or later, the sun rises. Weak rays poke through the trees ahead of me, a pallid light that snuffs out the glow of my nightgown and reveals trunks of standing pine as black and grey as if they were burned in a fire.

And I remember the fire and the smoke and the hot gasoline choking me.

I stumble, coughing, until I can breathe again.

There's no smoke here except for that which is rising from my skin, like spiderwebs, gossamer ballooning strands seeking the escape of the sky.

And the spiderwebs here are thick and numerous. As the sun continues its slow creep up through the trees, I wipe the heat from my arms and continue my slow walk forward into darkness.

Each tree is a monolith of dead wood. I don't know when the leaves disappeared, when life stopped greening, but I know I've reached the dark ridge because there is nothing living here. Tom and Eli said that no dead thing can abide in Ebenezer. This, then, must no longer be Ebenezer because death is everywhere here.

The only things living that I can see are bugs—and spiders. The path carries on, straight as an aisle in a church, between pines stripped bare of leaves, festooned with silk. In crevices and cracks, on limbs and in twisted roots, in tangles of fallen trunks, there are webs and watching eyes. Funnels like yawning mouths with hairy arachnids on their tongues, spiders as big as my palms, my whole hands, my—

I shiver, cold terror running down my spine. I have to turn back to the sun, the warmth, the bubbling waters of Ebenezer. To Tom who loves me and will always protect me, as I will always protect him.

What was I thinking, coming here?

I stumble, fall to my knees, get up again with webs stuck to my hands.

This, all of this, is what Tom is afraid of. This is why he never wanted me to touch the floating bubbles—not because they might take me to the meadow, but because they might take me, or us, or him, here. Here, where there are fearful things Tom can't control. Here, where…he's banished his fears?

I wipe my hands on my skirt, but the spider webs won't come off. They only grow stickier and stronger and stickier and stronger until my skirt clings to my hands, and I flap uselessly like a white bat. My feet—I pick them up to flee, but they snap back to the earth on webs as thick as woven corn silk. The wave of the ground swells toward me, a mass of spiders moving to consume their prey.

And I scream. I scream with the ferocity of certain death, with a full throat of fear and tears running down my face

And then, he comes.

a conversation

"You should scream," the Grey Man says. The spiders scatter at his voice, retreating so far into the forest that not a single one is left. "And you should cry, too."

Even the insects fly away, leaving a silent void into which he comes, through the trees, throwing shadows in his steps and casting them in his wake. He is himself shadow—the deepest shadow I have ever seen. A shadow that swallows all other shadows. Unbeing is his raiment and undoing is his path. He holds only the vague form of a giant man, towering over me.

I swallow my scream and dry my tears as best I can. He will not tell me what I should or should not do. I will be as obstinate to this...*being, person, thing* as I have life and strength to be.

Resist,
resist,
resist,
my heart beats.

He lowers his face to mine. "I am not here for you, but you are the reason I am here."

"H-here," I say through numb lips, "now?"

"*Here,*" he says again, so loud it shakes the drums in my ears.

And I understand what he means. Not here in this forest meeting my (foolhardy) challenge, but here in Ebenezer haunting Tom's steps.

He rises to his full height and steps back as if to consider me. "You don't know," he says in a voice that sounds almost kind. "Do you? I suppose that's why you've come. You think you can save him." He sits on a log, draws his legs up. "You can't save him. You can't undo what you've done."

"I haven't done anything to Tom," I say, feeling ill. "Certainly nothing to—to hurt him!"

The Grey Man leans forward, tsks his finger side to side. "There are no lies in Ebenezer, Beatrice."

"But I haven't!" I'm crying in earnest now. I cannot help myself. The tears roll stinging from my eyes and hot down my cheeks. "And even if I was lying, this isn't Ebenezer anymore, is it?"

"This is as much Ebenezer as every other place beneath this sky."

"But...there is death here!"

"Yes." And for the first time the Grey Man sounds pleased. "There is."

"Tom and Eli said that there couldn't be death in Ebenezer. And they can't lie. *You* said that, too. And I'm not lying either, and I will save Tom, and there's nothing for me to *undo* because I haven't *done* anything, I just—"

The Grey Man stands and grows. He grows as tall as the trees until he blocks out everything around us. I stand quaking, caught in the webs, unable to run away, even though everything in me is screaming.

"None of us is lying," the Grey Man says in a voice as big as the sky. "But that does not mean that we are all of us telling the truth."

"What does that *mean*?" I gasp, struggle against my bonds.

79

"It means I will take Tom and you will remember, or not. I do not care, and it makes no difference."

"Take him where?"

"From here." The Grey Man steps over me, in his hand appears the shape of a club. "He will come with me willingly, now that you have abandoned him."

"I did not abandon him! I came here to..." I can't say it—it sounds so ridiculous now. Ichabod was right.

"Yes," says the Grey Man. "What were you going to do, exactly?" He laughs. "Dim the lantern of your eyes, girl. There is no leading Tom from the fate you condemned him to. You put his feet on the path that leads through Ebenezer to me."

He strides beyond me with great, unhurried steps.

Knock,

knock,

knock,

he taps the trees with his club as he goes.

Renewed fear shivers down my spine. Tom is awake. Tom can hear him. Tom knows.

"But you're just *one* path out of Ebenezer!" I say, casting my voice after the Grey Man. "Aren't you?"

I close my eyes, picture the meadow with its warm green grass and its bright wall reaching to the sky. Not a wall, I realize now. A gate. It is as I first thought it was— a portal. I picture Eli standing over us, remember his soft feathers, the comfort of his wings.

The Grey Man pauses and the ground shifts beneath me.

When I open my eyes, the spider webs are melting, dissolving like frost. I brush them from my skirts and watch them float away. I take a step toward the Grey

Man.

"You are not the only way for Tom to leave. You are not the end of Ebenezer."

"He will never choose that path. You have broken him beyond repair."

His words are barbs, but I hold my ground.

"I will not let you take him."

The Grey Man returns in a rage, roaring violent steps that shake the forest as he swings his club at me. I crouch, but it passes through me like air.

I straighten and look him in his faceless face. "Love is stronger than fear and lives longer than death. You don't have any power over me."

"We'll see how you feel about love when he is gone," the Grey Man says.

And he leaves me alone in the dark.

help

"Dinah, help," I say. "*Help me!*"

I close my eyes to the dark forest and the blackened trees and the whisper of spiders returning. I can't possibly get back to Tom before the Grey Man finds him, but Dinah can reach me, even here. If she can only hear my voice.

"Help,

help,

help."

A rush of wings, and she is upon me. My feet leave the ground, and we are

up,

up,

up

through the trees, above them. I'm exhilarated, free. I can breathe again.

We rush on the wings of the sun back to the heart of Ebenezer.

i wish

A cold rain falls on Ebenezer. I tumble to the ground at the foot of Tom's treehouse, hoping he's inside. Praying he's inside and not hiding someplace else in the hidden places of the swamp. Someplace I may never find him, but the Grey Man might.

I can hear him knocking. He's close, and Tom is crying, afraid. The sky weeps and the ground trembles.

I don't dare call his name as I ascend the crossed trees to the base of the house, but when I push on the door, I find it locked. Locked. He must be inside. I tap my fingernail in a light, familiar query against the entrance. Too light. There's no response.

A window. I will enter through a window.

"He's not here," Minerva says, tawny feathers flashing through falling grey. "But you will find him first."

I shake my wet hair out of my eyes. "How can you say that? Where is he—do you know where he is?"

"He went to look for you, and that's where he stayed."

My hands slip on the bark of the tree as I cast my gaze over my shoulder. "My island? He went to my island!"

"He is there, and he is prepared to meet his end."

I release the tree and fall, expecting to land as I've grown used to in this place—light on my feet with the ground or the plants embracing me. *Their queen*.

Instead, I slam into the hard-packed path and lie blinking at the rain falling in my eyes, the wind swept out of me, back and butt and thighs crying out in pain.

Knock,

knock,

knock.

The Grey Man comes, nearer. He's here, searching, for Tom.

Get up.

I cough, I groan and roll onto my side. "What is happening?" I say.

"He is prepared to meet his end," Minerva says.

I roll again, this time into a sitting position. An insect buzzes by my ear—a mosquito that lands on my arm.

The magic is leaving Ebenezer.

I scramble to my feet and limp to the edge of the path where I lower myself into the water. It is cold and slimy, and I try to run, but the water is knee deep and my feet unsteady on the bottom, and I am drenched through already, so all I can do is slosh as fast as I can toward my island.

Dinah could take me. "Dinah?" I say, quiet, to not attract the Grey Man. "Dinah, are you still there?" But she doesn't come.

The magic is leaving Ebenezer.

Thunder rumbles and my breath leaves me in rapid, frosty bursts. I am sleepy, almost. Disoriented.

I have to find him. It's not too late.

Finally, my island rises out of the mist—a green sward in a grey cauldron. And he's there. I can see him curled up as if asleep, but his eyes are wide and staring.

I cry out in relief as I surge toward him. "Tom." I pull myself, sodden, onto the green bank and crawl to him, tripping and struggling in my skirts. I cast myself over his still body, touch his face, his cold cheeks. "I'm here."

"You came back," he says, lips barely moving, voice barely audible. "I thought you left."

"I went to the dark ridge to—to try to *help* you. But I was always going to come back! Didn't Ichabod tell you?"

"Ichabod said you went to see *him*. Ichabod said you left."

"I didn't leave. I'm right here. I promised I would come back. I would never leave you."

Away in the swamp, the Grey Man moves among the trees. I can sense him getting closer.

"We have to go, Tom, quickly, before he finds us. I'm sorry I—I didn't know—" No, I can't say that. It would be a lie, and it chokes and dies in my throat. I *did* know that going to find the Grey Man could draw his attention to Tom. Ichabod told me, but I refused to listen. I thought I could beat him, but now I see, and now I know who and what he is.

"It's too late," Tom says.

"It's not too late!" I'm desperate, pulling on his arms, his shoulders, but he lies like one dead. "You can't let him find you. You can't let him take you. I love you."

Tom lets out a long breath that sounds like his soul leaving his body. Warmth flows from his mouth and melts the frost that has gathered on his lips and on the grass pressed to his face. White lilies unfold from the ground, pushing up through the soil in a little mound. Color flushes his cheeks and he sits up, stilting himself

85

on shaking arms.

"I love you, too," he says. "I've always loved you—since before this place. Outside, inside, and ever after. You are my Queen Bea. I would follow you...here, there..." He frowns. "Anywhere."

"Then follow me away from here."

Voices rise in the air around us, voices as desperate as my own. Tom shudders and the sky tears apart with lightning. The Grey Man laughs as he comes.

"You have delivered him to me. My wait is over."

"Again."

"We're losing him."

"Stay with us, Tom."

Voices jostle and tumble over each other, and lightning strikes again, this time piercing the clouds, the trees, the Grey Man—who lurches back.

The lightning skitters along the surface of the water, sparkles that refuse to fade. It chases back the shadowy grey beast until he stands far from us, looking in on our little spit of land.

"You can't touch him," I say, though my teeth chatter with fear. "He will come with me, and you can't touch me. I stand between you."

"It doesn't work that way!" The Grey Man grows until he fills the sky. "You have no power here. You are an interloper, a traveler, unwanted and alone. You don't even know who you are!"

"No, but I know who you are," I say. "I name you"—I raise a shaking finger, breathe courage into my chest—"Death. You may have come for Tom, but I have come for you."

The Grey Man laughs again, but I take a step toward

him.

"You call me an interloper, but the real interloper is you. You don't belong here, and you don't make the rules of this place. Tom has banished you to the farthest reaches, along with all the other things he is afraid of."

"He hasn't banished me anywhere. I am and will always exist."

The ground tilts under us, sending the Grey Man tumbling head over feet farther away from us still.

"There is no lying in Ebenezer," I say.

"He can't get rid of me." His voice comes fainter. "That power does not belong to him. He doesn't get to choose his fate."

"Maybe not. But he can remember." I finger the hard stone tied into the hem of my skirt. "I can help him remember his life, and what it holds. And that life is always stronger than you are. That you are dreadful, but you don't get to choose his fate, either. You are broken, and his story is not over."

I turn my back on Death.

The Grey Man rages, but Tom is standing now. His eyes are bright, his hand slides warm into mine, his feet are wide and planted. Around us, the swamp comes alive with budding flowers orange and yellow and white as the sky splits open.

I tear the stone, the wishing stone, from the hem of my skirt and hold it up between us. I trust in Tom's power as the king of Ebenezer to transform an ordinary stone into a wish. I trust he made me truly his queen.

"I wish," I say, "that we would remember everything that brought us to this place. I wish that we would be made whole."

remembrance

Twisted metal, a burning cage of fire and smoke. I can't breathe. Sirens beat against my brain, in darkness. I—

Upright, driving down a sunny lane, singing at the top of our lungs, trailing a carefree hand out the window. I grin at Tom, and he beats his hands on the steering wheel. We—

Lying in a meadow, honeybees buzz in halos around us. We wriggle our bare toes and I wrinkle my nose, sneeze against a blade of grass, tickling my face.

"Cut it out," I say, but Tom laughs his impish laugh and tickles me some more.

"They like you... That's what I'm going to call you from now on," he says, pointing to a bee that lands on my shoulder. "Bea!" His voice is light, high, youthful. We are young, cheeks round, limbs plump with muscles unrefined.

I smile and hide my face in my bushel of curls, try not to let him see my blush. "Better than *Beatrice*."

"Any name is better than Tom. Plain, boring Tom."

"I think Tom is a nice name. I think—"

Twisted flowers into a crown, which Tom places with wide-eyed concentration onto my head. He twists my hair around my crown and smiles to crinkle the corners of his eyes. We are again in our meadow. Older now, but not by much—gangle-limbed and stretched and large eyed. *We are between.*

"There," Tom says. "Now you are *Queen* Bea."

I don't hide my blush. I lean forward with concentration, intention, inspiration in a moment of firsts.

Firsts. We brush our lips, he says—

"It's only a bruise."

"Tom."

His shoulders, hard and straight, marching ahead of me, parting the waves of students in the hall.

"Tom, look at me!"

"Look at me, look at me!" Mocking voices parrot me. Laughter, mean as the mark on his skin. "Yes, Tom, *look at me*."

A boy on the football team with hair like Jason's fleece and a neck and arms thick like Ajax slams Tom into the water fountain. He cries out and drops his books as the hallway erupts in cheers.

"Get to class!" A teacher's voice. Never enough.

"*Look at me*," I say, with tears.

He looks, his eye, black and blue.

"It's just a bruise, Bea," he says.

"It's not." I trace his dear-to-me face. "They hate you because you love me. Because I love you. Because I *chose* you."

"Beatrice." The headmistress, hard and stern. "Your mother called. She wants you to come straight home after school today. No clubs or..." Her hard eyes wander to Tom. "Anything else."

"Ma'am." I stand and straighten my uniform. Plaid skirt, polo, penny loafer shoes. "Do you see what those boys have done? Do you even care?"

"Beatrice Grey Magnolia Grange, how *dare* you say such vile things? Of course I care about Tom. We all care."

"Then help him! Stand up for him. Do something about what is happening here." I grasp the shoulder of his hand-me-down shirt, feel the thread-bare fabric

94

stretch beneath my desperate fingers.

Headmistress purses her lips in her way. Folds her hands and says, "Come along, Tom, to the nurse with you."

He shuffles to obey, eyes down, head down.

I say, "Headmistress—"

She says, "Beatrice, there are some families we just don't—"

"Beatrice, Beatrice, follow me! We'll go to our swamp and together be free!"

"I don't think a *swamp* sounds very free." I slap bugs off my baby skin. No, I'm older than a baby, but not by much.

We run through dandelions, chase grasshoppers through bobbing plants, dodge red mountains of fire ant swarms.

"But this isn't just any ordinary swamp. This is my swamp where I will be King, and I will make the rules, and I will say that we will rule together!" He laughs and spins in a circle a circle a circle until he is breathless and laughing and falls on the ground. I fall with him.

"What will we eat there? Pizza? Cookies?"

"Nothing. I don't want to have to cook. It's a magic swamp kingdom where no one is ever hungry."

I don't have to cook because we have a person who does that. So I say, "I think it would be lovely to eat honeysuckle. *Magic* honeysuckle. Haven't you ever had honeysuckle, Tom?" I roll over in the grass, thinking of perfect summer days.

"'Course I have. Okay, yes, you can have magic honeysuckle if you want it. But you don't need it." He flaps his hands. "Not in our swamp kingdom."

"Can we have servants in this kingdom?" I say.

"Sure! What kind?"

"How about..." I flop onto my chest and think thoughts a child would only think. "A squirrel!"

"Okay! We could name him Archibald."

We laugh because a squirrel named Archibald who is a swamp servant is silly indeed.

"And a mouse—a mouse! Please, can we have a

mouse?"

"A mouse named Shiloh," Tom says seriously. "How grand."

"Why Shiloh?"

"Why not? It's a name I once read. And how about also"—he gets a wicked gleam in his eyes—"a snake!"

"Ew, Tom, no."

"We can't have a swamp without a snake."

"Sure we can, if it's our swamp."

"I *insist* on a snake."

I wrinkle my nose. "Fine. But only if it's a magic snake, that can talk!"

"Beatrice!" My name, from my mother's lips, calling from the big white house with the big white fence and the horses and the acres of land across the lane.

"I have to go," I whisper. "Tomorrow? After school?"

"Only if we get to go to our swamp," he says.

"Deal."

We grin, and shake on it, and I scamper across the road. The heat rises from the baked pavement like smoke from a grill on the Fourth of July. I hop along the white stones bordering our drive and dream of building a new world with Tom.

"Bea!" Tom calls after me.

I turn, shade my eyes against the sun. Shield his pillbox house.

"I like you most of all!

"I like you, too. You—"

"You can't date, and that's final. What will people think?"

We hold hands, fast, in the foyer of the great white house. Shaking and shivering from some dip in the local pond. Found out, dragged here. Together.

"I...don't care what people think." I shiver, hiccup. "What does it matter?"

"Don't be naïve, Beatrice. It matters."

"Why? Because we're rich? Or because he's—" I look at Tom, standing tall beside me, skin brown and bright in the light of the entryway windows.

"You should not suggest such vulgar things," my mother says, voice low and hissy, hand to her heart.

"I didn't suggest it, you did."

A slap, across my face. Stars. "Who do you think is paying for him to go to that school with you? You should be grateful—both of you."

"Mrs. Grange, I—"

"Get out of my house, Tom."

I can't see him for the tears in my—

I trace the pocket on his school blazer—finger the threads coming loose. Pick them out one by one and let them go to float on the breeze like dandelion fluff. We give him scraps and expect him to praise us for our benevolence.

"Run away with me."

"Where would we go?"

"Anywhere. Everywhere. Not here."

Tom rubs his curly head and stretches beneath the sun. "That sounds nice, but I would also like to graduate. Wouldn't you?"

"Who cares about graduation? I hate seeing you in pain every day. The way those boys torture you..."

Tom is still beneath me. "I'll survive, Bea. It's only one more year."

"My parents know we're still dating."

He chuckles, sardonically. His chest rumbles beneath my cheek. My favorite rhythm. "It's kind of hard to hide. You've been coming over here since you were five."

I raise myself to look down at him, stretch my brow into a serious line. "I'm worried they might pull your scholarship."

"Well, if they do, I'll...figure something out. Take a job."

I scoff. "Enough to pay tuition?"

"Then I'll go to public school like everyone else." He shrugs. "People do it every day."

"But your momma—your poor momma. This is what she wanted for you!"

He tugs on my dangling curls. "And you want me to run away."

"Not *really*." I flop to the ground beside him. "I just want you to be happy and safe."

"I am always happy and safe as long as I'm with you."

We twine our fingers and listen to the breeze through the bending oaks. A horse in our pasture whinnies and our dog barks warning of a car coming up the road. We—

Hold hands to hold each other up. We are twelve—
an uncertain age. A man in a grey suit knocks on the
door of Tom's house. Three times. Peers through the
front window. Knocks three more times. His car, parked
in Tom's driveway, reads, "County Coroner."

"Tom, what is a co-ro-ner?" I say. "And why won't
he go away?"

"I've seen him at the hospital," Tom says. "He tells
people bad news." Tom's hand goes loose in mine and
he moves toward the house.

"Don't go! You aren't allowed to talk to strangers
when your dad isn't home and your momma is in the
hospital!"

"I think"—Tom swallows, he doesn't look at me. "I
think this time I have to talk to this stranger."

"Then I'm going with you. It's my job to protect
you." I flash him a smile. Anything to make my Tom
smile when he's blue. But Tom only has eyes for the man
in the grey suit.

We emerge from the forest like wild things looking
for scraps, and the man starts at our appearance.

"What do you want?" Tom says in a voice that
doesn't sound like a question.

The man casts his eyes around the house, the
meadow, across the road. *No*, I think, *there are no more of
us.* It's always been just me and Tom.

"Son, where is your father? Is anyone else home?"

"He works late on Tuesdays."

He works late every day—or goes straight to the
hospital to be with his wife, but there's no need to tell
this stranger that.

"Who is watching you?"

Tom shifts from foot to foot, so I say, "We are. My family watches him. We live across the road." I point.

"Well, then, are your parents home?"

"Not right now, no sir. My mom went to the store."

The man in grey opens his mouth.

"She'll be gone for a long time."

He mops the sweat from his pale brow, casts his eyes around again. "Well, Tom—it is Tom Smith, isn't it?"

Tom nods.

"The hospital has been trying to reach your father, but we've been unable to get through. We—"

"They don't let him take phone calls during his shift," I say, loud and aggressive. "Don't you know that?"

"Well, little miss, I guess I didn't—" The man looks from me to Tom. He kneels, with effort, his grey suit stretching tight over knees that crack. "Do you know who I am, Tom? Why I'm here? It's about your mother. She—"

Tom runs. He wrenches his hand from mine and runs across the meadow, fleeing death or the certainty of it. He runs toward the forest and the swampland beyond—the swamp we play pretend is our special kingdom.

"*Tom!*" I take off after him, young feet pounding old earth, but he has been faster than me for several years. I'll not catch him unless he wants to be caught.

He disappears into the verging trees, where birds take off in fright. Deep in the swamp, he hides his tears, but he cannot hide his scream.

"Get in the car."

"I've got this."

"No, you don't! Get in the car, we're leaving!"

"*Bea*."

"Tom, I have to get you away from here."

"Why? Because these are your people and not mine?" He stands, silhouetted against the football rally bonfire, skeleton-like in the orange light and smoke. Another player throws a beer can at him and jeers. He doesn't duck fast enough, and it hits him in the shoulder.

"I didn't say that! That's not true, and you know it. I just—I'm so sorry we came. I love you. Let's just go!"

"Let me handle this on my own. I'm not a helpless baby, Bea." He pushes past me, approaches the jeering crowd.

"Just run away, Tom. Run away!" Tears stream down my cheeks as I stand, pleading by the open door of my car.

"Yeah, run away, poor boy. *Freak*." A push, a shove. Tom sprawls in the dirt. "Nobody wants you here. I bet your mom died 'cause she didn't want you and your dad works such long hours because he can't stand being around you. And everyone knows you're not good enough to date Princess Beatrice Grange. My dad says they talk about you at the club—'bout how you're an embarrassment to the whole town. They would've torn your house down years ago if they coulda got it condemned." A harsh laugh, a swig of beer. "If you call *that* a house."

I can't fight these ghouls that masquerade as boys, but I charge forward and gather Tom into my arms and say, with quiet wrath, "I am no princess. I am a *queen*.

103

He named me. You are nothing compared to him, and you will not talk to us again."

Hoots and howls, like the cries of demons, pursue us as I help Tom, stumbling, to my car.

"Let's go," I say.

He nods. Defeated. Done.

I wipe my eyes and smudge my tears, pull to the county road. A watercolor painting of dark and light and bends and curves. The car rumbles beneath us as I sit in indecision.

"Where would you go," I say to Tom, to the chiaroscuro world, "if you could go anywhere—right now?"

"I wouldn't go anywhere in this world, in any world, without you," he says.

"What other worlds are there?" I wipe my eyes again. I can't see the way I want to see.

Tom sighs, heart deep, drops his head against his window. He closes his eyes. "Let's go to our swamp. Do you remember the one?"

Our swamp, the place of make-believe from when Tom and I were young and free. "Okay, let's go there."

A rock hits my back window. Laughter chases us, closer.

My sight isn't clear, but I don't need clarity to hit the gas, I—

Don't see the truck. Tom's head meets headlights and glass like a hammer, shatters. We fly, off the road,

roll,

roll,

roll,
into a tree. And—

Wake suddenly to twisted metal, a burning cage of fire and smoke. I'm on fire and I can't breathe. Sirens beat against my brain, in darkness.

I can't breathe,

I can't breathe,

I can't breathe.

I grope for freedom, gasping against lungs that won't fill. My fingers find the button that releases me, and I fall, and I cry, and I reach for him, but he isn't moving. He is limp, dangling like a belt on a loop, bleeding like a squeezed orange, silent like death.

But death isn't silent, *it screams*.

"Stop screaming, Beatrice, you sound like a lunatic. Can't someone give her something?"

"Ma'am, step back."

I can't stop. I won't stop until they tell me—

"Don't you tell me what to do. I'm her mother. Don't you know who I am?"

"I don't care who you are—she's my patient and you're in my way."

A nurse, a flash of feathers, no, hair, as she leans over me.

I breathe, speak, "Tell me, please, is he—?"

"He's not dead. He's here with you, at the hospital."

"*Dying*?"

"There's nobody that can say that but God."

They only say that when death is at the door. The scream is inside my head now. "My... fault. Driving..."

"Hush, child. Was no one's fault. You rest and heal. It's time to sleep."

My veins...cool and heavy, but my skin, on fire. I—

remember

my fault

Remember.

Everything. Life. Our life, together, and the life we hoped for. All the pain, all the joy, all the love, dreams, and fears.

It was not easy. Maybe it was harder than most, but who can say? We only walked in our shoes.

Tom raises tremulous, tear-filled eyes to mine, and I know that he was in our memories, too. He is no longer a feral drus, but at home, with me.

He folds his long fingers around my fist, closed like a beating heart around the stone of remembrance. "This was just a stone," he says.

"It is a wish because you said it is a wish, and you are the king of Ebenezer."

"I...I am..." He looks beyond me to the Grey Man, who waits, silent now. Bound by our command. "Dying."

"You are *living*." I take his face and turn it back to my own. "Look in my eyes, Tom."

He does, and we see each other.

"This whole place is alive because of you. Ebenezer is you, don't you see? You brought our special place to life."

"You think we're...in my mind?"

"I don't know where we are—I just know that a dead person couldn't do this, and one who wanted to die wouldn't bother. You've faced so much pain, and I—" The sob catches me off-guard, cinches my throat. "I—I'm sorry."

Tom frowns. "For what?"

"For everything that's ever happened to you. For how my family treated you. For...the car accident. It was my idea to go to that rally. My fault, that we crashed. He is right, it *is* my fault—"

Tom crushes me to him in a hug that melds our bodies and souls. "It is your fault that I have never ever been alone. Your fault that I have always been loved. Your fault that I'm...*alive*." He lifts his chin to set it on my shoulder. Says in a low voice in my ear, "Run away with me, Bea."

I sniff and straighten until we breathe the same air, nose to nose.

"Run away with me. It's time to go to our meadow."

He looks at Death and says, "No." And then he turns his back and slings his arm around my shoulders.

My arm, around his waist. My head, against his arm. We step in tandem back into the warm water of the swamp and tread our way to the path.

he is gone

The distance is shorter, somehow, as if Ebenezer knows we are on our way out. Or— more probably—the land is conforming to Tom's will. As it's always done. We pull ourselves onto the high path, crawl up onto it like children, laughing at each other and flinging water droplets that sparkle in the sun.

Following at a distance like a whipped dog, is the Grey Man. We know he's there—he knocks the trees and mumbles accusations—but Tom has set his face forward now.

We leave the swamp, pass through the forest in long strides, journeying fast. Running, I guess. But we are not winded. The meadow lies before us, a great wall of white light at its edge.

"Do you see it now?" I say. "The light."

"I see it," he says. "Has it always been there?"

"As long as I've been here."

"So, you could have left...at any time."

"I could never have gone anywhere without you."

"I will divide you, in the end," the Grey Man says, imposing himself. He's caught up to us, but he doesn't draw near.

Tom and I clasp hands and move into the meadow, putting our bare feet to the green grass.

"I come for all people." His voice changes now, into a different voice, a new manifestation. No longer the Grey Man—he's talking to me. "Someday I will come for *you.*"

I do not turn to see what form my psyche has made him. "Someday," I say, over my shoulder. "But not today. Today, you are banished from Ebenezer."

Tom takes another step toward the light and looks back to where Death was. "Look, Bea," he says.

The dark ridge is bathed in warm light. Behind us, all the animals we've ever known have gathered, as if to say goodbye. Death is nowhere to be found.

"Do you think—" I say, but my hand grasps air, and I look down, then up, then all around. "Tom?"

He is gone. He is—

the king and queen of ebenezer

"Well, look who's awake!"

Beeping, soft and consistent. Am I awake? I don't feel awake. I feel...asleep. Groggy. I grope for my arm. Tubes. My face. More tubes.

"Easy, child. Easy. It's just oxygen. Give me a tic."

Movement around my face. Adjustments I can't see.

Was it a dream?

No.

No.

My eyes, slow and sluggish. I grasp the tube in my nose and pull it out.

"Alright, alright. You don't want your oxygen. Let me just make sure your levels stay up."

Kind hands, kind words. Helping me.

"I am—" My throat hurts, doesn't want me to speak.

"Shhh... No need to talk. You've been asleep for a long time. Let me talk for now, and you can nod." The woman, the nurse, smiles. "And since you *are* awake, I have good news for you. Can you handle good news right now?"

I nod, but already I'm crying and smiling because I already know. "Awake. Alive," I say. "*Tom.*"

"That's right!" The nurse sits back. "Now how did you know that? He woke up just an hour before you. Been asking about you ever since. 'Course, we told him you never were in any real danger. Not like him." She moves out of my sight.

"See?"

114

"You want to go see him?"

I nod.

She comes back, purses her lips. "Probably should get the doctor to check you first, but..."

My eyes travel to her nametag: "Minnie." I point with a weak hand. "Minerva?"

She looks at me, startled. "Yes. How on earth did you guess—?"

"See—Tom. Please?"

"Yes. Yes, okay. I'll call for a wheelchair."

I close my eyes and wait, and when she returns to my side, it's with a nurse with a chair and a nametag that reads, "Dinah."

"Now what's this? How did this get in your bed?" Minerva picks up something from my blankets, turns it over in her fingers. "A *rock*?"

My chest swells and I hold out my hand, hardly able to get out my plea. "Don't...throw it...away!"

"Okay, okay," she says, placing it in my eager palm. "Although why you would want a dirty river rock is beyond me. You kids these days. Come along now."

She and Dinah transfer me to the wheelchair, and as Dinah pushes us out into the hospital hallway, I look up at Minerva and say, "Thank you."

"For what, baby girl?"

I clear my throat, every moment feeling stronger. "For watching over me."

She smiles, presses her hand to my forehead. "Child, it's what I do. Follow me—I'll take you to your boy."

Tom's nurse, Eli, meets us outside his room. "Did you get approval for this?" he asks.

"I think forgiveness might be better, in this case."

Eli looks at me, looks into the room behind him, and then waves us through with a smile that says *he knows*.

Dinah parks me beside Tom and then steps outside the room, leaving us alone.

Tom's head is wrapped in bandages, but he's sitting up and his eyes are keen and bright. We look at each other for a long time, just to see what new eyes see on waking.

Then I take his hand from where it rests on his bedspread, and I open his fingers and press into them his wish.

He turns it

over,

and over,

and over

and smooths it with his smooth fingers, and he whispers through chapped and disused lips, "Not over after all."

And I cry because some tears are for joy. And we clasp the wish tight in hands that will not let go. Together, the king and queen of Ebenezer.

about the author

K. B. Hoyle's love of good stories began when she stepped through a wardrobe at age six, and she never looked back. She is the multiple award-winning Young Adult author of *The Gateway Chronicles* and *The Breeder Cycle*. She stays busy at her home in Wisconsin on a winding creek with her husband, their four sons, and the array of wildlife that frequents their land.

For more information on K. B. Hoyle, visit her website at kbhoyle.com or find her around social media at @kbhoyle.author on Instagram, Facebook, or Threads. Connect with her via email at author@kbhoyle.com.

acknowledgements & special note

The Queen of Ebenezer is a book that has been knocking around in my mind for several years. It was probably back in early 2017 that I took my first notes on the story. 2017 was a year of grief for me, and I had no idea how grief would chase me—would chase us all—as we edged into 2020 and beyond. I was living at the time in Alabama, just down the road from a swamp called Ebenezer, and the pathways there became a thin place for me. A place for me to walk, be mindful, think, pray, dream, imagine, and grieve. It was both dangerous and safe—hushed and filled with sounds of things I couldn't see. It felt like a place out of a story, so I decided to put one into it.

But I'm glad I waited as long as I did to write this story, because I wasn't ready to write it in 2017 or any of the years between. I hope I was ready to write it now and that what I've put between these pages is beautiful! A very special thanks for this book goes out to Ash Schlax and Katie Stewart, my dear friends and editors who have loved this story so well and come alongside me to help it shine. Thanks also to Michelle Moran for your generous and beautiful cover painting of Ebenezer Swamp. And to all my wonderful people at Owl's Nest who are helping self-sacrificially with all the work of publishing and promoting—this book and all the rest—thank you always! Beth Anne Dunphy, Lindsey Pearce, Ally Castaldo, Timarie Friesen, Elizabeth Hance, and Carol Foust.

Thank you for reading this Owl's Nest book! We hope you enjoyed it. Please consider leaving a review on Amazon, Goodreads, or sharing about the book on social media!

You can find and follow Owl's Nest Publishers on social media by searching for @owlsnestpublishers.

Find extras, merch, our mailing list, our podcast, and other great middle grade, teen, poetry, and classic books at owlsnestpublishers.com!

Find cover artist Michelle Moran at michellemoranfineart.com

This is the Owl's Nest; come in and read!

9 781957 362243